Quickies – 1
A Black Lace erotic short-story collection

Look out for our themed Wicked Words and Black Lace short-story collections:

Already Published: *Sex in the Office, Sex on Holiday, Sex in Uniform, Sex in the Kitchen, Sex on the Move, Sex and Music, Sex and Shopping, Sex in Public*

Published in May 07: *Sex with Strangers*

Published August 07: *Paranormal Erotica* (short-stories and fantasies)

Quickies – 1
A Black Lace erotic short-story collection

BLACK
LACE

Black Lace books contain sexual fantasies.
In real life, always practise safe sex.

This edition published in 2007 by
Black Lace
Thames Wharf Studios
Rainville Road
London W6 9HA

O	© Nuala Deuel
Life Boat	© Virginia St George
Doctor's Orders	© Jessica Donnolly
Pumps	© Monica Belle
Lovely Cricket	© Jan Bolton
Kissing the Gunner's Daughter	© Fiona Locke

Typeset by SetSystems Limited, Saffron Walden, Essex

Printed in Great Britain by CPI Bookmarque, Croydon, CR0 4TD

ISBN 978 0 352 34126 6

The Random House Group Limited supports The Forest Stewardship
Council (FSC), the leading international forest certification organisation.
All our titles that are printed on Greenpeace approved FSC certified
paper carry the FSC logo. Our paper procurement policy can be found
at: www.rbooks.co.uk/environment

O Nuala Deuel

Inga Loeb was single because she wanted to be that way. She had no shortage of potential suitors, but her independence meant more to her than any number of proposals, any number of velvet boxes from Alexandrov; vows of love and fidelity tumbled over and away from her, as ephemeral as the windstream across an aeroplane's wings.

Inga was an air stewardess; she worked exclusively for a Saudi Arabian businessman with his own Lear jet. It was just one more reason she could offer to the pack of randy dogs that were chasing her tail. *I can't have a boyfriend*, she'd say. *I'm on call twenty-four hours a day. At any moment I might be expected to drop everything and fly out to Europe, to South Africa, to the States.* Her boss, known to everybody as Ali – to recite his entire name would take a good fifteen seconds – was a hard taskmaster, but extremely fair. He smiled at Inga often, and chatted to her when he wasn't working on his laptop, or calling clients from 40,000 feet in the air. It was important to her to know that she was more to him than some kind of drink-fetching robot. He asked her opinion on various matters. He confided in her. Sometimes her duties extended to errands that took place on the ground: purchasing gifts for special clients, checking out hotel facilities for all-day conventions, arranging dinners at short notice at elite restaurants. She had a certain amount of persuasive power, and knew that these gifts were more likely to work if she could utilise them in person. She was an attractive young woman, with glittering green eyes and an hourglass figure that she liked to squeeze into sheer black dresses and high heels, or, when she was relaxing, expensive scuffed leather trousers and thin clingy tops. She turned heads, and she often made them nod too, whenever she asked for something to be done. She was not used to rejection.

For such an inconvenience, she was paid handsomely. She enjoyed a top-end five-figure salary with regular, generous bonuses, and owned a large studio flat in Bayswater and a modest terraced house in Devon, which she decamped to at every opportunity. She had a good circle of friends and an interest in photography, world cinema and jazz.

She was also addicted to online shopping for sex toys.

Inga loved the anonymity of such shopping. She loved too the little routines she had developed on the nights she decided to settle down for some retail therapy with the mouse and the Mastercard. There was always a hot bath first, and a large glass of Rioja. The sash window she slid open as wide as it would go. Miles or Bird or Dizzy on the stereo. Candles. She immersed herself in the hot scented water and closed her eyes to this blanket sensual infill. When the glass of wine was finished, she would feel a little thick, a little woolly in the head, a sensation echoed in the pit of her stomach. Her mind would be turning to silicone and steel, to leather and lubricants. Her long hair fanning out in the water, washing up on the floating bounty of her breasts.

Tonight, on the eve of her thirtieth birthday, she reached for a bar of lavender soap and ran it along the gulleys at the side of her body, where the flesh swept down to the pout of her pudenda; the many nerves bunched beneath her flesh here singing as they awoke to her intent. She pulled out the bath plug and felt the water lowering. Her weight drew her down as the bath emptied. Her pubis broke free of the surface, like an exotic sea creature caught out by the tide. She ran the soap over the hair there, enjoying the lather as it thickened, feeling the cream slither into the frills of her labia. She squeezed her thighs together, and the sight of her long limber muscles becoming defined under her skin, enhanced by the oily light, turned her on more than she expected. She was sleek. She was a thoroughbred. More of her body became exposed as the water gurgled away. The deep curve of her waist. The nub of her belly button. Her breasts settled back against her ribcage proud and perfect, like something cast by a sculptor eager to capture her in her moment of glory. She watched her breasts shudder as she worked the soap against her cleft, creating so many suds now that it was difficult to keep a grip on the bar. The sound of the soap as it sucked and squelched into her quim was deliciously rude. The last of the water gathered in an eddy at the black O of the plug hole and she watched it spin wildly away. She reached down to the low table by the bath and swept up a brightly coloured configuration of moulded jelly and plastic. She flicked a switch and the head of its seven-inch shaft rotated. A separate, bifurcated offshoot vibrated alarmingly. She thrust the vibrator into her pussy, as deep as she could get it, and positioned the buzzing clitoral arouser against her hot little flood button.

Fifteen pounds from *www.honeypot.com*. A bargain.

She came before she could find a rhythm to move against, ploughing the firm silcone into her with fervid abandon, imagining a man crushing her against the enamel surface of the bath, his own senses lost to the pooling of heat that gathered at the tip of his monumental cock. The vibrations were deep and intense. They always produced a different kind of orgasm to the one she experienced with her fingers. It was as if every single nerve ending was being attended to at once by the little machine. It was mind-blowing. Quite often she had a headache after playing with one of her toys; they were that thorough with her. Yet, as had happened now in the empty bath, her skin puckering as she cooled, she had not been able to reach her climax without thinking of real meat pinning her down. Her toys were all about preparation; they couldn't deliver the coup de grâce. Ultimately, despite their sophistication and their lifelike appearance, it was the lack of humanity that failed her. The sound was too mechanised; the smell too synthetic. She loved the rhythm of sex, the measured slap of flesh.

It was like the beat of the drums in jazz, it created the spaces within which the music happened. But she could never find the toy she needed to replicate that. And no matter how hard she worked them, there was never the reciprocal sound of a lover losing control: all of these things were what drew an orgasm from her. It wasn't all about direct clitoral stimulation.

Still, she loved the naughtiness of her machines. There was a thrill in using something that was custom-made for the vagina, and for pleasure. Hanging around a businessman for as long as she had, she couldn't help thinking that there was a gap in the market, but she couldn't imagine how it might be filled. All she could do was keep trawling the websites until that border between the actual and the pretend was smudged to the point where it no longer became something worth considering. Tonight she would find herself a toy worthy of a woman entering her fourth decade. She wanted the best there was, and she would not call a halt until she had found it.

Inga rose shakily to her feet and pressed her fingers lightly against her mons. A residual tremor existed there. She was still excited and by the time she had reached her bedroom and jiggled the mouse to chase away the screensaver, knew that she was going to have to trawl the web one-handed. But not to some grinding background of white noise. She dumped the vibrator in her under-wear drawer and reached for the beautiful, thick twelve-inch glass dildo she had bought in Amsterdam the previous summer. It didn't gyrate, it didn't throb, and it had a tendency to feel a little chilly, but that was what she craved right now. She sat naked on the office chair in front of the Apple Mac, her legs spread, cunt tilted towards the screen, sliding the end of the dildo all over her fizzing, swollen pussy lips.

She clicked through her bookmarked favourites, enjoying the gentle slip and slide of the tool as she slithered it tenderly across her opening, not yet wanting to fuck herself into oblivion. The filed list of sites that she had previously patronised seemed suddenly too pedestrian; she wondered if she had taken her proclivity too far and become jaded: nothing on the pages aroused her as it once had.

She desultorily ordered some strap-ons because she liked the colours and the quality harnesses. She bought some large steel cock rings of various diameters and a few of the lifelike vaginas, just for fun. But none of it was connecting with that little zone in the pit of her stomach, the place that was like some secret internal mouth forever locked in an O of surprise and arousal.

She grew bored of her usual haunts and typed a few key words into the search bar. *Lifelike*, *sex toys*, *ultimate*, *realistic*. She realised that what she was actually looking for was a man as soon as she hit the return key, but by then she was too engrossed by the jags of pleasure ramping through her clit to consider what this meant. She spread her legs even wider and eased the bulbous head of the glass into her. The shaft of the dildo was a beautifully shaped series of concentric circles, like thick ribs, and she felt each one as she swallowed the fat glass, inch by inch. Her pussy lips rippled around the girth of the dildo. She felt filled up, stretched. The tip nudged up against her cervix and a low moan shifted wetly around the base of her throat. She began to slowly pump the glass cock in and out of her drooling quim as the search results came back. In a daze, feeling her control dwindle, she glanced down the familiar list of names, most of the links coloured red to indicate she had visited them before. There was one website that had escaped her attention, which surprised her:

www.o.com.

It must be new. She clicked on it, imagining the dark eyes of her imperious ghost lover peering intently into her own as she bore down on the orgasm waiting to be hatched inside her.

David.

She felt herself tip over that invisible edge and had to put out her hand to steady herself as the legs of the chair she was sitting on skidded back away from the table. Her release was a like series of circles that rippled away from that tight little nub of pleasure at the top of her cunt. Whenever she felt her orgasm, she thought of the old RKO sting that appeared before movies, of radio signals buzzing from a mast on top of the world. She imagined the peristaltic spasm of a ring of muscles desperate to squeeze the ecstasy from her body because it couldn't hope to stay intact if they remained behind.

She came back, as she always did, despite the conviction that each climax sent her further away from herself. Reality poured into the gaps of her in the shape of her credit card, the mouse, the chirrup of her computer as it processed any number of little unseen tasks.

'Hi, Dave,' she said, thickly. Her heartbeat felt visible in the skin of her chest. She was exhausted and energised at the same time. The homepage of *www.o.com* contained nothing more than a picture of a male sex doll that was so lifelike she thought it might turn to her and tip her a wink at any moment. Short hair, a cute mouth, chocolate-brown eyes. His body was a pale caramel colour, his prick tumbling halfway down his thigh, soft, but with a heavy weight to it. It had real presence: it drew the eye. Next to the picture, in acid pink lettering, were the words:

> Meet Dave. A six-foot tall hunk of hard muscle and good loving. Made with the highest quality materials. Watch his erection grow as you caress him. Realistic thrusting action. Realistic ejaculations. Awesome sucking and tonguing programmes. Listen to him tell you how great you were afterwards. A stunning piece of equipment, the ultimate sex toy for the discerning woman. Buy now.

How could she not? Despite its four-figure price tag, it was a piece of kit that she must not ignore.

She quickly entered her details and punched the transaction processing key. A few seconds later, a screen appeared thanking her for her order and informing her that her purchase would be with her in three working days. She drained her glass of Rioja and swept back to the bathroom feeling suddenly revitalised, somehow like a teenager again.

As she showered away the sticky residue of her climax, she imagined it was because, in a way, she had set up a date. It was like being sixteen again, at college, waiting impatiently for the Friday night and a movie with the class Adonis. Three days was an impossible time to wait. She felt herself shiver in anticipation. Plenty of time to pamper herself. To make the treat something more than it was.

She went out for a walk.

The streets around her home were glossy with long-departed rain. The sodium lights were caught in the sheen-like holes punched in the skin of the Earth, allowing glimpses of wondrous lands beneath. These merged with the smeared windows of countless flats rising to her right. She had been walking for so long she was unsure of where she had arrived at. The windows shivered with pulses of TV colour. Some of the glass was shrouded by net curtains. Others allowed an unhindered view of the rooms inside. She wondered about the people sitting in them. How many of them were about to have sex, or had just finished? How many were in the middle of the act right now? She remembered teenage boyfriends honey fucking her on parents' sofas in front of the television, for hours sometimes, once the frenzy of the first few occasions had burnt itself out. Lovemaking changed, she suddenly realised, as you grew older. You knew how to fine-tune. You knew exactly what you wanted, and how to extract the sensation you craved. There was no longer any hit and miss, any wild abandon. Control was what gave adult sex its frisson, but it was also what stripped it of its magic too.

As if summoning some evidence to the contrary, she turned her head to catch sight of a couple in a kitchen, fucking in the buttery light from an open refrigerator. He had her against the worktop, thrusting into her as her hands slid against the MDF, her eyes closed, her breasts juddering, the nipples proscribing crazed parabolas over their soft heavy background. The couple's domestic setting, the easy knowledge they had of each other's naked body, the way he peppered her chest, throat and face with kisses instructed her that her beliefs were flawed. There was surprise on the woman's face. And the thrill of it was there too; she had been ambushed by him. A smile surfaced, turning into the frown of sweet excruciation, breaking into a smile again as she reached the limit of feeling. She opened her eyes and fixed Inga to the spot. She hugged her man close to her and Inga felt the acres of cold night sky pile in on her. She had never felt so separate, so isolated. At home she had hundreds of pounds of diversion.

By the time she arrived back at her flat, she was so despondent that she could not bring herself to get undressed. She dropped to her bed as the clock on her computer softly chimed the hour. Midnight. Now she was thirty.

Inga awoke to a sound like a flock of birds. She experienced a moment of depression when she saw that she was still dressed in the previous night's clothes. A couple of jelly dongs stood to attention on her bookcase next to a tube of self-heating lube and a pair of padded nipple clamps. A day of glorified wanking lay ahead. She could have anything she wanted, from the slimmest, stubbiest four-incher to the mammoth eighteen-inch pole vault that she needed to take muscle relaxants for. The thought of all that impersonal, meatless meat exhausted her before she'd even flicked a switch.

I need a holiday, she thought, at the same time understanding that she didn't know what she wanted; yet more, that she did, but she couldn't put a face to it.

She traipsed downstairs to the source of that avian sound: a stack of birthday cards on the welcome mat. The sight of so many tributes from friends cheered her and she spent the next quarter of an hour tearing into them. A cup of raspberry leaf tea and a bagel later and she felt more sanguine about her position. Everyone went through a phase of self-doubt. Everyone who masturbated had to swallow a little guilt, a little self-loathing, however misplaced.

She cheered herself up further by remembered friends from college who had been brazen in their enjoyment of themselves: Anna who would always play Madonna's 'Justify My Love' to indicate to others that they must not enter her bedroom for any reason; Kim, who loved to come on all fours, using all of her fingers, rilling them across her vulva like an anemone sifting the sea for titbits; Madeleine, the French exchange student who greased her mons up with groundnut oil and climaxed by squeezing her thigh muscles together with such skill and precision she could manipulate her clitoris while her hands dealt with the hypersensitive flesh of her nipples.

Those times had been good for her not only because she had a steady stream of friends on tap, but they helped to open and close certain doors in her life. She could remember kissing Madeleine on the doorstep at midnight, summer clinging to the blue-black sky, their faces so damp with perspiration they had grown bored of wiping it clear and had let it come. She had tasted of salt and apples. The kiss had been exciting because it was unexpected. It was the first time she had drunk chilled Beaujolais, or eaten fruitcake with Wensleydale cheese. It shouldn't work, but it did. Was that brief flirtation with lesbianism – a kiss, a breast's tip in her fingers, a nervous, trembling thigh pressed between her own – the reason she had not linked up with anyone now? Despite her confidence, the hunger to be a success in her work, was she essentially someone who didn't know anything?

She thought she might cry, or smash a glass, or get roaring drunk. In the end she did none of these things, and merely sat in the centre of a circle of greeting cards, watching for the shadow at the window of something that might take her away from herself, even for a little while.

The knock at the door was almost too tired to rouse her from her sleep. She lurched for it, her desperation shaming her. She signed quickly for the package, so much larger than she was expecting, unable to meet the postman's gaze, in case he was aware of what it was she was receiving. Once she had closed the door, she left the monolith of brown paper and parcel tape and hurried to the kitchen, where she poured herself a large brandy, downed it in a few swift gulps.

She couldn't believe he was actually here. She imagined him uncomfortable and stifled in his packaging. She quelled an irrational stab of panic. He was a toy. *It* was a toy. His penis curled against his thigh, perhaps taped to it, to prevent it from becoming prematurely gorged. His balls. She imagined cupping them, lifting them, measuring their soft weight. She might take one of them, or both of them, into her mouth, feel the underside of his cock twitch and throb against her nose . . .

She approached the package, which was leaning, almost nonchalantly, against the sofa. She imagined his voice: *Here, perhaps? Or upstairs? You decide.*

She feverishly unwrapped him, yanking him clear of his bubble wrap and shrink wrap, tossing away the yards of cardboard, twisting open the plastic ties, freeing him from his unedifying bonds. She stepped back. He was hunched over, as if in thought. His hair, when she haltingly reached out to touch it, was soft, real. Suddenly she was gushing, setting free words that she had never spoken, never imagined she would ever say: *I love you. Will you marry me? I love you. I love you.*

She started to cry, both in gratitude that she had been able to purge the entreaties from her system, and in disgust of her need, at the weirdness that was rushing into her life. She wiped her eyes and pushed him back onto the sofa. She was mildly shocked at the feel of his shoulder muscles; there was yield but there was also – *God how could there be?* – resistance too, as if he had thought for a second about denying her the satisfaction of bullying him. He lay, not like something synthetically rigid, but with relaxed presence, his body observing gravity's laws. His arm flopped naturally over the edge of the sofa. His head was tilted back, revealing the cartilaginous ridges of his throat. She watched, rapt, as his left leg, hooked over the armrest, moved to the rhythm of a heartbeat. It must be hers, fooling her, surely they wouldn't go to so much trouble?

He said, 'You're beautiful.'

There was the slightest suggestion of digitisation to the voice, a minuscule click at the start and end of the sentence, but it was a relief to hear it. She had begun to believe that a real body had been dumped on her doorstep and she wasn't sure how she might deal with that. The spookiness of the situation receded; this was a doll. A very good toy, but a toy nonetheless. She let her dress fall to the floor.

'David,' she said, her voice thick with anticipation.

'Yes, darling?'

She reached behind her and unhooked her bra. 'It's time to get my money's worth.'

The phone rang towards early evening, as she was slowly putting together the ingredients for a dinner she didn't want.

'Inga, hi. It's Cass. Ali has been called out to Milan. An emergency meeting concerning the hostile bid for Judd Janeway. He's expecting a series of negotiations. Could go on for two, three days. The jet is prepped and on standby. Sorry it's such short notice. There will be a car with you inside twenty. OK?'

The names of these companies were like phrases of foreign languages heard in passing. They meant nothing to her. She knew Ali was into as many companies as there were fingers on his hands, perhaps as many as there were rings on his fingers, but none of them rang any bells. It was part of a world she didn't understand, or hoped to fathom. Venture capitalism, in the main. Which sounded to her like a fancy term for opportunism. Get rich quick. Good luck to him. It was obviously working. Was it a coincidence that he was single too? Like her he claimed it was what he wanted to be. But maybe like her it was a question of protesting too much. Sometimes people never asked the question, and she told them anyway. Too often, recently, when she said it it seemed more like she was trying to persuade herself.

For the first time in Ali's employ, she wondered about him, about her and him. Was there some alchemy between them, on a level she had yet to unveil? Such a scenario seemed too convenient, and too Hollywood, in a way. The driven businessman and his help, at different ends of the food chain, yet inhabiting the same space, sharing the same life, give or take a million or two.

She had never seen Ali with a woman, had never

even spotted him appraising female clients, or the girls that moved sinuously within his striking range on the streets of Manhattan, Prague or Barcelona. There were ample opportunities for him to sate any pang, yet she had never paused in her knocking on the door of his hotel suite at the sounds of passion from within. It never happened. She had never had to divert the queries of an inquisitive husband, nor, for that matter, any inquisitive wife. Ali seemed to be asexual. It was as if any dalliance with another person was somehow wasteful in terms of time; he was more interested in spreadsheets than bed sheets.

Inga had never really considered him in these terms before, either. Perhaps because she had been unknowingly put off by his neutrality, but possibly because he did not spark anything visceral within her. He was an attractive man in many ways; he was lean and wolfish, with hooded eyes and a full mouth. His hair was slightly longer than the conventions of his career permitted, and its blue-black gloss was shot through with seams of silver. He was unusual looking, and therefore sexy. But his lust for profit had turned his features into something that was beyond what could be construed as predatory in sexual terms. He had the killer in him. She had heard him laughing over a competitor's liquidation. For him, fucking was something to be done metaphorically, and only ever in the ass.

The car, with its tinted glass windows and inscrutable driver, whisked her through the rain-soaked streets of West London. On the Westway, as the great glass edifices of the Paddington Basin streaked by, she felt a prickle of anger towards Ali, the way he summoned her whenever he wanted, as if she were something cryogenically suspended at those times when she wasn't fetching and carrying for him. Her life was not on hold when she wasn't working, despite the handsome payments that bolstered her bank account. For the first time since taking the job, she felt resentment.

She closed her eyes, breathing deeply. Things were coming to a head. And that was good, she reasoned. Questioning her position meant that something wasn't right somewhere. The money was good but the karma wasn't. Perhaps this was an indication that she was about to make choices based on who she was and what she wanted, rather than what everyone else demanded from her. That was the key to making the break from childhood. Being yourself. It was just that, for over twelve years, that was all she had done.

Her cunt ached. Whenever she moved, his smell rose from the apertures in her clothing. Slices of action from the day flashed into her thoughts, like stills from some forbidden portfolio. She reached down and massaged her pussy through her uniform.

'You have beautiful breasts ... I'd like to suck them.'

His mouth opening, his eyes swooning shut: her nipple disappearing between his ice-white teeth, the leading edge of his tongue settling against her tit. His lips pursing, drawing her nipple to a taut exclamation, rolling it around his mouth.

My God. It was so real. It was real. She had laughed out loud.

Rising to his feet as she knelt on the sofa, his hair falling over his eyes. Holding his penis as it thickened, peeling back his foreskin to reveal the swollen shape of his desire. Her vagina suddenly slick with juice as she realised such a beautiful, huge, sculpted prick was seconds away from filling her up. The feel of the tip squirming against her folds, almost sliding off her. The inches. The light tap of his balls against the top of her thighs at the end of that delicious first strike. His breath on her spine. The thrust, the sensation of being unravelled as he partially withdrew, as if the organ were no more part of her, than him. The cushioned spring of pubic hair. Her name in his throat as he quickened. His hand encasing her breast, palpating her, squeezing pleasure from her pores.

My God, my God.

Her orgasm burst out of her as she reached around to feel his hard quivering buttocks clenching with the force of his own. She felt three, four, five hot silky spasms deep within her. He withdrew and liquid pearls frothed from her crease. She dabbled her fingertips in it and brought them to her nose. Fresh seed. How did they manage that? She glanced down at him; he was sweating, his skin flushed. His erection was subsiding, but she had knelt and sucked and licked at him, marvelling at the taste of his semen, enjoying the way that her ministrations were reviving the corpse of his penis. He was hard again within a minute. She slurped at him, giving him her entire repertoire of kisses, flicks and nips, enjoying the way he filled up her mouth, the way he groaned and ground his hips against her face. She sucked him hard and fast, than let him fuck her mouth slowly, barely touching him with her tongue and lips, providing the merest amount of friction. Then back on with the full throttle, then easing off. He was writhing. He came in the middle of another bout of frenzied sucking and she was impressed that the quantity was less this time. The manufacturers had omitted no detail.

She had left him on the sofa as the car drew up outside. 'Sleep well, David,' she said. 'My David. We'll be together again soon.'

Now she came again as her fingers writhed in the slick created by her memory, her legs rising, feet knocking the chauffeur's headrest. She could barely stifle her cry, and decided not to. She didn't care if the driver saw her. As she froze in the instance of her climax, she saw his eyes in the rear-view mirror, her own face behind it, her mouth a red-rimmed O of surprise and elation. The tide receded; she blew him a kiss.

'Tell Ali,' she said. 'Tell him what you like. If he fires me I'll thank him for it.'

A twinge of shock, of fear, of disbelief, as she stepped from the car at Heathrow and headed for the departure lounge. Don't look back. Do not look back.

Two hours later, she was exhausted. She had been busy with pre-flight checks and had served Ali aperitifs and dinner shortly after take-off. Now Cass was briefing her on the itinerary once they landed in Milan. She couldn't concentrate. All she could think of was David. She realised she had made a decision. She was going to leave her job. She had never felt tired at work before, and it wasn't solely due to David's athletic lovemaking. Her tasks were tedious. The thought of carrying on like this for even another week, let alone another year, made her feel sick to the stomach. As Cass talked of hotel lunches, guest lists and corporate goody bags, Inga was reminded of the chauffeur. A spike of panic ripped through her. His voice, as she stepped clear of the car, had been bracketed with a little digital click, as had the captain's just now. At least he had an excuse, speaking through the intercom. Or was she just imposing little bits of David on to the humdrum, trying to spice up that which could no longer be enlivened?

Cass materialised by her side. 'Ali would like a word,' she said.

Was it the change in pressure as the jet sank towards Milan that caused her voice to sound metallic? Inga suppressed a giggle. She needed a holiday. First chance she got, she was off to the beach. With a *very* large suitcase.

Ali was ensconced towards the rear of the jet, behind a series of heavy curtains. His desk was piled high with papers requiring his initials. He processed another dozen of these before lifting his head and indicating she should sit down.

'I understand you've had a change of heart regarding your career path?' he asked her. His hooded eyes never looked so raptor like. She felt like a morsel being proffered by a bird handler.

'How did you ...?' she began, but he held up his hand, his eyes closing slowly, as if to say *You don't know me by now*? 'Yes,' she said, firmly. 'I've worked for you for a long time. I think it's time for a change.'

He nodded. 'And which job is it that you're tired of?'

Inga blinked. 'I don't understand.' She spread her hands. 'This one. I'm tired of this one.' The first needle of doubt. Fear was in this cabin. It was trying to place a suffocating mask over her face.

'Not the other job then?'

'I don't have another job.' Her heart was beating too hard. As if part of her knew what he was talking about.

Ali stood up and walked around the desk until he was closer to her than at anytime during her employ. He unbuckled his trousers and let them fall to the floor. He was naked underneath. She felt the cabin sway, the lights fade. For a second she thought the cabin had succumbed to some mechanised fault and was pitching out of the sky, but then everything righted itself and she saw that it was only the sight of Ali's cock, of David's cock, that had taken her to the brink of fainting.

'I don't ...'

'No. Clearly you don't,' Ali said, pulling up his trousers and leaning back against the desk. 'There's a reason why I keep the details of my businesses secret from my employees. But now that you're handing in your notice, I'll share it with you. I own a number of companies, but my main interests are in the synthesis of the best elements of the human and the machine. That and sex. Sex is the most ancient of businesses, flesh and metal hybrids the most modern. I like that. I like the balance. The poetry. All of my sex toys are modelled on me. Even David. Your boyfriend. How does it feel to know you've been fucking your boss?' He smiled. 'You've tested lots of models for me over the years, and I'm extremely grateful. I doubt we'd be where we are now if it wasn't for your exhaustive research into dildos and dongs.'

'That wasn't my job.' She could barely speak now. Alarm signals were blaring all over her mind.

'It *was* your job,' he said, moving towards her. He placed a hand on her shoulder. 'But now your contract has been terminated.'

She felt his fingers at the back of her neck. She made to speak but her throat could produce only a click. She felt something snap.

Her vision shrank to a small white O. Nothing.

Nuala Deuel is the co-author of *Princess Spider: True Experiences of a Dominatrix*, and has had short fiction published in numerous Wicked Words collections.

Life Boat Virginia St George

The ship was an old-fashioned cruiser with a dress code at dinner and seating plans in a glass case in the hall. Breakfast was served on the pool deck under canvas umbrellas. Sunlight glinted off the artificial blue pool and dark-green ocean – light thrown back like shattered glass. The waiters, busboys and bartenders all wore white uniforms complete with gloves. In the lounge, sequined singers still sang the old songs: 'It's a Wonderful World', 'Never on a Sunday'.

For her high school graduation, Lauren's parents had brought her to Greece. Athens. A bus tour of the Peloponnesus. A week-long cruise of the Mediterranean. At night, she stretched across the old springs of her berth. She thought about sex, love and the future. She imagined her future, herself at twenty-five, an ad exec or lawyer in expensive high-heeled shoes and tight leather pants, a woman who would fuck men and be gone in the morning. She felt so naïve still, on her first trip to Europe, so soft and girlish despite her best efforts to become world-weary and wise. She longed to be a heartbreaker.

The third evening of the cruise, at the dinner table with her parents, Lauren found herself next to an

English doctor and his pretty wife, both dressed in white linen. Also at the table were American siblings, in their third month of a year of travelling, they said. 'We're from Utah.' The sister was rosy and dark-haired.

'Are you Mormons?' Lauren raised an eyebrow.

'Oh, no, we despise Mormons. I hope there aren't any on this ship.' The sister looked over her shoulder and giggled, displaying a small gap between her front teeth. The waiters appeared and with a flourish removed the shiny metal covers from their platters in unison.

Lauren studied the brother. He was wearing a sand-coloured corduroy coat with leather elbow patches, unseasonably warm attire. His face was freckled, even his eyelids, and his hair was sandy like his coat; he didn't look at all like his sister. There was a tattoo on the inside of his wrist that peaked out from under his cuff as he struggled with his cutlery: 'INCONCESSUS AMOR' in cursive script.

'What does your tattoo mean?'

'It's a secret.'

The dining room was grand, chandeliered. At the other tables silver-haired gentlemen poured wine for their smiling, round wives. Retirees. Older professionals on summer holiday. The sounds of clinking china and silver was a polite cacophony.

'We're the youngest people here,' Lauren said.

The brother raised his eyes from his swordfish and brushed his hair from his eyes. He smiled. 'I'm Ben. She's Casey. Call her Cass.'

Cass's eyes glittered. 'Have you noticed the wait-ers? They're young. All male too.'

Lauren blushed and glanced nervously at her mother.

Cass shrugged. 'Don't pretend you didn't notice.'

Lying in her berth listening to the heartbeat thrum of the engines felt like sleeping inside a body, warm and close. Lauren felt the slow rocking of the sea, nestled in the ship's dark depths, cradled in its womb. Before she slipped into sleep, Lauren touched her clit softly, stroking it while thinking of Ben and her ship full of young men.

When Lauren woke late in the morning, her parents had already gone above deck. She put on her bathing suit and a sundress, then, glancing in the mirror, raked her fingers through her hair. Good enough.

The elevator up to the pool deck was empty save the elevator operator.

'Up to breakfast?' His face was tanned and freck-led with sun. His dark eyes stood out against his white uniform. He glanced at her, just for a moment.

'Yes.' Lauren stood behind him as he pressed the button with his gloved finger. The doors closed. The young man's hands rose again and he pressed another button. The elevator stopped suddenly. He turned to her, and put his wet mouth over hers. His face was pressed so close to hers, all she could see were his dark eyelashes over his closed eyes. She could have counted them if she'd wanted to.

The soft fabric of his gloves grazed her thighs. He tasted like coffee, his tongue bitter and forceful inside her mouth.

She gasped for breath. I could fuck this guy, this nameless guy, she thought. He wants me. He could give me pleasure. For a few moments, I could be the centre of his universe.

The elevator attendant pulled his hands free of his gloves and grabbed her ass as he pushed her up against the wall of the elevator, grinding his body into hers. He fingered the elastic edges of her bathing suit. Lauren could feel herself getting wet, responding to him. He groaned as he pushed his hand into her bathing suit and found her asshole. Lauren cried out as he pushed a finger inside her. It felt lovely, but dirty. It made her hot, but it felt wrong.

'I have to go, my parents are waiting for me.' She pulled herself away from him.

'Please.' He was panting and his eyes were pleading. 'Please?'

'No, I've got to go.' Lauren pulled down the hem of her sundress.

He grabbed her wrists and pushed them around her back. He kissed her again, forcing his tongue deep inside her. Her heart raced with fear and arousal.

He pulled away from her fast as the coppery taste of blood filled her mouth. 'Fuck! You bit me.' Lauren smiled at him, his blood on her teeth.

'Crazy bitch.' He pressed a button and the elevator began to move.

At breakfast, Lauren drank coffee and the cup shook in her hands.

Around noon, Lauren found Cass sunbathing topless on a deckchair next to the pool. Her breasts were milky compared with her round, tanned shoulders and arms. Cass had a fashion magazine covering her face. Lauren thought she was beautiful like this, exposed, embracing her own exhibitionism.

Without removing the magazine, Cass said, 'I'm driving the wait staff completely wild with desire.' Cass's skin glistened with tanning oil and the smell of coconut mingled with sweat wafted off her. She peeked out from under the magazine pages. 'Do you want to join me?' Cass tugged at one of the ties hanging off Lauren's swimsuit. 'Did I mention that I'm doing a tour of the men of Europe? I've yet to land myself a Greek. On this ship I've already had a Hungarian. Did you see him? Tall man, salt-and-pepper hair? Wears the red Speedo bathing suit for his swim each morning? His body is hard as rock.'

Lauren smiled and shrugged.

'Oh, don't be coy. Everyone notices The Hungarian.'

'I haven't.'

'Oh, well. I have a plan, if you'd like to be in on it. To land myself a Greek. A busboy would be good. They look like they would be so appreciative, don't you think? You can have one too. We'll meet here after dinner. Wear something that shows some skin.'

* * *

In her cotton tank top and skirt Lauren felt rather unglamorous beside Cass's low-cut red dress. 'I always wear red when I want to just ooze sex.'

'You look nice.'

'You do too. In a sweet, wholesome way.' Cass's eyes moved away from Lauren's body to a young man crossing the deck with a tray of empty glasses.

'Hey, you there. Busboy?' The young man turned and looked questioningly at Cass.

'Come over here for a second. I'm looking for a bottle of ouzo and I don't want to order ouzo drinks all night. I want a full bottle. Do you know where I might be able to purchase such a thing?' The busboy had to struggle not to look down Cass's cleavage as she bent towards him. 'Do you have a bottle? Or a friend who has one? Could I meet you later to buy it from you?'

The busboy looked wide-eyed and overwhelmed for a moment, then shook his head yes. 'Ten minutes, yes? Cabin two-six-five? Both of you come?' Cass smiled, her teeth white against her scarlet lipstick. The busboy turned on his heel and jogged away with his tray of glasses tipping perilously.

'Well, he's cute and he understands English pretty well. I reserve the right to choose him until after we've seen what his friend looks like. It was my plan, so I get first pick.'

'Why would he bring a friend?' Lauren liked the idea of an adventure, but buying a bottle of ouzo seemed unlikely to yield a thrill, let alone score a busboy.

'You'll see. Now that we have ten minutes to

kill, let's see if we can't do something about your outfit, OK?' Cass led Lauren towards the elevator.

Cass's cabin was a mess of clothes hanging off the edges of the berths, the chair, the bathroom door. Giant bottles of duty-free perfume cluttered the small vanity. Cass pulled a sequined dress off the chair and offered Lauren the seat.

'You share this room with your brother?'

'Unfortunately. But he knows enough to keep all his things in his suitcase. I travel in style as you can see. I get it from my mother – she was an actress. I think Ben must have gotten his neatness from his dad. He was an accountant.' Cass wrinkled her nose playfully. 'Mother's fourth husband. She really does have a voracious appetite for men. Now she's on to husband number six.'

Cass opened a drawer, which overflowed with make-up, cigarette packages and small bottles of booze like the ones served on aeroplanes. 'I'm thinking black eyeliner for you. Maybe a spritz of Opium. And this.' Cass pulled a backless chiffon blouse out of a lower drawer. Lauren peeled off her tank top and felt Cass's eyes on her body, her gaze sliding languidly over Lauren's shoulders, breasts and stomach.

As Lauren slipped on the blouse, it felt light and luxurious against her skin. 'Now you feel as sexy as you are.' Cass ran her finger slowly down Lauren's neck, from her chin to her collarbone. 'Do you feel sexy?'

* * *

Lauren and Cass found the busboy, a friend and an open bottle of ouzo waiting for them in cabin 265. The curtains were drawn over the portal. The room was immaculate, obviously uninhabited. The two boys wore matching uniforms, and even their well-shined black shoes were the same. The friend had eyes that slanted up at the outside corners and showed sharp white teeth when he smiled. I want that one, Lauren thought.

'Good evening, boys.' Cass danced into the room, spreading the scent of her perfume as she moved. 'What do we have here? A little private party?' Cass grabbed the bottle of ouzo, walked into the bathroom and collected four Dixie cups and began to pour. 'Classy.'

'Hello.' The friend made room for Lauren beside him on the berth. Cass looked him over slowly as Lauren sat beside him.

'So, boys, what signs are you? Let me guess. I'm good at this.' Cass handed out the cups. 'You look like a Scorpio. Am I right? And you – a Leo?'

The busboy smiled awkwardly and shook his head.

'I'm wrong? You're not a Leo?'

'Myself, I am a . . . a crab?'

'Ah, Cancer.'

'And was I right about you?' The slant-eyed man shrugged, looked helplessly at his friend and said something in Greek. 'Oh, well. I guess he's yours. No English.' Cass smiled, showing her teeth, then picked up her drink and proceeded to sit in the busboy's lap.

'What's your name?' Lauren blushed as she looked at her companion for the evening.

'Christopher.' He moved towards her and brushed her lips with the tips of his fingers. 'Beautiful, yes?' He held her cheek in the palm of his hand, rough and warm against her. 'Kiss?' Lauren closed her eyes. As he moved closer, she could smell the scent of him, the slight smell of bleach from his uniform, sweat from a long day's work. She couldn't help wishing she could breathe his air, suck in his breath, sweet and wet against her mouth.

She gently bit his lip, plump and full like a ripe plum. He put his hand on her breast, then slipped it into the open back of the shirt, around to the front, and pinched her nipple. Lauren gasped as pleasure pulsed through her body. She could feel herself getting wet, just from a kiss and playful touch.

She put her hand on to his cock, feeling its stiffness through his pants. He wanted her. She could feel it in the electricity off his skin, the way he held his breath when she touched him.

'Listen, boys. This is all well and good, but I've got to tell you. My friend here, she isn't just my friend. She's my lover and watching you touch her makes me jealous.' Cass was standing in the middle of the cabin, towering in her high-heeled shoes. The busboy started talking rapidly in Greek to his friend. Lauren looked up at Cass with a question mark in her face. 'I want you to take your hands off my girl.' Cass pulled Lauren up by the hand.

'Two girls? Lovers?' The busboy's forehead was wrinkled with confusion.

'You do have lesbians in Greece, don't you?' Cass pulled Lauren to her and kissed her on the mouth, then moved her mouth towards her ear and licked her earlobe. The kiss was wet and sensuous and Lauren wanted more of it. Cass whispered into Lauren's ear, 'Not fair for you to have the hot one. I want them both.' Lauren stepped back and looked at Cass: there was a mocking mirth hiding around her eyes. Cass drew back and slapped Lauren across the face. It stung only slightly, but Lauren was shocked by its suddenness, its utter unexpectedness.

'Whore! You're making me jealous on purpose! Why would you do that to me? I want you out of here. I don't want to have to look at your face.' Cass was a queen of melodrama, her voice sing-song, her movements exaggerated, her emotion filling the room. She pushed Lauren towards the door and out into the hallway and then promptly slammed the door.

'Cass, I...' A question hung on the end of Lauren's tongue as she heard Cass lock the door from the inside. Lauren's body was buzzing. She felt strangely hollow and confused. She'd only sipped the ouzo. Lauren could hear Cass's giggle through the cabin door. Greedy, insatiable Cass. In that kiss, Lauren felt as if she had been given a clue, a way to possess the woman she wanted to become.

Lauren felt the sting of cool night air as she came up on deck. The expanse of stars and water – the vastness of it – made her feel as if she might explode out of her skin, like an astronaut outside of her spacesuit. Ben's dark shape reclined on a deckchair, eyes glittering, the cherry of a cigarette orange between his fingers.

'You seen Cass?' Ben ashed over the ledge of the deck, into the sea.

'No.'

Lauren settled on the edge of a chair and reached for the lit cigarette. She put it to her lips and took a drag, letting the smoke sting the back of her throat. Ben was Cass's brother, but Lauren could make him her own in a way that Cass never could.

'You don't smoke. I can tell by the way you hold it.'

'So?'

'So, it's a nasty habit.' Ben took a pack out of his shirt pocket and shook a cigarette from it. 'And, if you are going to do it, you may as well do it elegantly.' He put the cigarette in his mouth, lit it and then let the smoke stream effortlessly from his mouth into his nose. 'Let me teach you to French-inhale.'

Lauren sucked smoke into her mouth, then opened it slightly and breathed in through her nose. Smoke rose around her head like a halo. 'Like that?'

'Don't open your mouth so much.'

Lauren tried again.

'Better. But remember it is supposed to be sensual.'

'So I should half close my eyes and try to look like Marlene Dietrich?'

'If it helps.'

Lauren glanced up at his face. Amusement bent the edges of his lips. She leaned towards him and put her lips against his mocking mouth. She would not be coy. Not any more. What was the use of it? It was better to take the man you wanted. It was better to want than to be wanted. He tasted like salt and smoke, but his mouth was soft and warm against hers. She put her hands on his chest and felt the heat of him through his shirt, the hard muscles of his chest, the buried beating of his heart.

'What are you doing?' He moved his face away from hers.

'I'm kissing you.'

She kissed him again, pushing his lips apart and finding the wet centre of him. She ran her hand down his chest, across his stomach and down to his hips. Her fingers lingered on the sliver of bare skin just above his belt buckle. A silky patch of hair ran between his navel and his buckle and, as Lauren stroked it, she could hear Ben's breath falter.

'We can't do this here.'

'We'll find a place. We'll both look around and meet back here in ten minutes.'

This is it, she thought to herself, this is finally it. I will vanquish him and leave him in the morning. Anticipation prickled against her clit, like the throbbing engines far beneath her. Weak, silly boys never had a chance – they were just the fodder for her lust. She watched his ass as he walked towards the front of the ship.

* * *

When he returned, Ben was flushed with running. 'I've looked everywhere. Up there is an empty space where there are just ropes and stuff on the deck, but it's open to the sky. I don't know if there is a place.' Ben leaned on the railing, giving up. 'If you don't really .–'

'I thought of a place.' Lauren pointed.

'Overboard?'

'No, look behind you and down.'

Ben looked over the edge of the railing, and then looked up at Lauren. He smiled, and his teeth shone white like a Cheshire cat's.

It was a calculated leap between the rail of the upper deck and the roof of the lifeboat. Lauren scrambled down on to the narrow deck and tried the hatch. It was open. Inside, the air was warm and heavy against her skin, moist and fragrant with diesel, dust and salt. The space was lined with padded benches and the small windows let in only a dim light that made the interior black and white. A hidden space.

Lauren clutched Ben's shirt by the collar as he followed her into the cabin. She pulled him close and kissed his lips as hard as she could. She would have liked to taste him, if she could have, taken a bite of him. She crushed his body against her own. She needed to get closer. She fumbled with the buttons of his shirt.

'Wait, a sec, I –'

'Quiet.'

Lauren unbuttoned his shirt and slipped it off him. She got down on her knees to unbuckle his belt. The buttons of his fly were difficult and she had to slide her hand under the waist of his jeans. She pulled the denim down from the knees and let the pants settle around Ben's ankles. He stepped out of the pile of fabric, leaving his flip-flops behind too. Ben's boxer shorts were a light, clinging fabric that almost stuck to Lauren's fingers as she pulled them down. In the dim light, his skin looked silvery and his pubic hair was a dark patch of shadow. His body was sinewy and long, and she could see his tattoos in their entirety, a phoenix that stretched across his upper back and sent plumage down one arm. She traced its contours with her fingertips and he shivered under her touch. Ben moved his head to kiss her.

'Wait. I just need to do something.' Lauren ran her hands down his back, feeling the fine hair beneath her fingers. She caressed his muscular legs, his knees. She felt the generous proportions of his buttocks. She smelled the back of his neck, the nape of his hair. He smelled faintly like heat, the memory of sun. She licked his earlobe, it tasted like sweat.

'OK, now kiss me.'

He grabbed her, hungry, and clutched fistfuls of her hair as he kissed her. He pushed her down on to the bench and peeled off the chiffon top and cotton skirt. He smiled at her when he found that was all she had on. Lauren looked down at her naked body, appraising it as she thought he might. Narrow hips, small breasts, but strong and taut. His mouth found her nipple and she gasped. It almost tickled.

His fingers left a trail of fire down her belly to her cunt. They felt big and rough as they moved against her clit. Unfamiliar. Unpredictable. She moved against him. She closed her eyes. Her entire consciousness moved down into her pelvis, the slippery movement of his fingers, the wetness of her cunt, the longing to be filled up with him.

She found his cock with her hands, judged its hardness, its girth, with her touch. Very hard. Shaped like a stick of dynamite and at its tip there was a piece of metal. Lauren opened her eyes. The tip of his cock was pierced with a ring with a barbell on it. Lauren tugged at it gently. Ben sighed.

'Ben, I want to fuck you.'

Ben pushed her knees apart with his legs. He kissed her as he guided his cock into her cunt. She moaned as the tip entered her. Ben pushed his hips into her and his cock slid deep inside her. Pain and ecstasy. Friction and heat. Lauren moved against Ben, rubbing her clit against his pelvic bone. She was getting sweaty and her slick belly slipped against his. The pain made her catch her breath.

'Does it hurt?'

'Yes.'

Ben whimpered in ecstasy, his breath fragmented, broken up with pleasure. Lauren could feel the tension growing in her cunt, coils of energy pulling tight against the walls of her vagina. She sank her nails into Ben's shoulder. She moved against him, faster, harder. She could feel her juices dripping down between the cheeks of her ass. She could feel his breath, staccato, against her neck. She could feel his cock deep inside her, filling her up.

And then, for a moment, her mind went blank. There was a small explosion inside her. A flash of white light on the backs of her eyelids. I am the whore of Babylon, she thought. The fucking whore of Babylon.

'Oh, my God. Oh, my God.' Ben was moving inside her. In and out. Faster and faster. She felt a burst of warmth inside her and he collapsed on to her, sweaty and drunk with pleasure. He pulled his cock out of her and his come ran down between her legs on to the bench. Lauren reached down and touched it with her finger, so slippery. She brought her finger to her mouth and tasted it. Like the sea. He lay beside her, cupping her breast in his hand, face tucked into the crook of her neck.

'I know what your tattoo means. The one on your wrist. I asked my mom – she studied Latin. It made me think you might be a romantic. A Romeo. Are you?'

'I have my romantic delusions, I guess.'

'Have you ever been in love?' Lauren asked.

'Yes.'

'What's it like?'

'This isn't it.'

'Good.'

There was a silence.

Lauren slept and dreamed of home. Of the greenness of home, the boys who smelled like their mothers' clean laundry, the girls fated to marry. She dreamed of her high school sweetheart and his tenderness in the back seat of his car.

When she woke, it was light and Ben was gone. She could hear laughter and conversation on deck.

The clinking of glasses. Shit. She slipped into her clothes, opened the hatch, and peered up at the deck. She clambered on to the roof of the lifeboat and pulled herself up over the railing. Breakfasters turned and stared, teacups held halfway to their lips, forks frozen in the air. She knew how she looked, dishevelled, sleepy-eyed, a stowaway. A matronly woman with tight white curls pursed her lips in disapproval. A red-faced man laughed for a moment.

'Your young gentleman made his escape almost an hour ago. Didn't expect that he'd had a companion.' The man's eyes crinkled into tiny slits with depraved delight. You're all voyeurs, Lauren thought. Perverts. She curtsied exaggeratedly, before turning towards the elevator to the lower decks.

Lauren stopped in front of Ben and Cass's door, beige with gold numbers, identical to all the other cabin doors on the whole ship. She knocked. How could Ben have left her alone in the lifeboat? *She* was supposed to leave *him*, lonely in the morning light. She knocked again. Jerk. She tried the doorknob and, when it turned in her hand, she pushed into the room.

On the bed, Cass's enormous naked breasts jiggled as she writhed against the white sheets. Sweat stood out on her collarbone, her hairline, her upper lip. Between her legs, Ben lapped at her clit, one hand reaching up to Cass's mouth, where she sucked on his fingers, the other holding her ass. The embrace wasn't familial. Cass's pinkly round and supple body was passionately enmeshed with Ben's long and sinewy paleness.

Lauren stood stock still, waiting for the image to make sense. For a moment, she wanted to join the wicked, moaning, quivering union and be one with the sweat and the bliss. Lauren looked at Ben's naked back, his phoenix, which only hours ago had belonged to her. Traitor. Ben looked up at her, his mouth shiny with Cass's juices.

'Where are you from, Lauren?' Ben didn't bother wiping his mouth.

'Toronto.'

'We'll check that off our list, then.'

Cass giggled as she pushed Ben's head back down into her cunt. Only then did Lauren notice the words 'INCONCESSUS AMOR' tattooed on Cass's hip. Forbidden Love.

Virginia St George's story, *Life Boat*, appears in the Wicked Words collection *Sex on the Move*.

Doctor's Orders
Jessica Donnelly

She pulled back the curtain and stepped forwards briskly, as she liked to do when meeting patients at the hospital for the first time. It made her feel like she was filling the role her white coat demanded of her: authoritative, confident, a woman in charge. She trotted out her familiar line: 'Hi, I'm Dr Cooper, how can I help?'

'Hello, Emma,' he said.

For a second, she was thrown. But then even before she had the chance to look at him properly, she knew who he was. That voice. Jon Adams. Third year at university.

'Jon! What a surprise! I –'

'Didn't expect to see me?'

'God, no, I – how are you? I mean, what's the matter?'

'Well, Doctor, it's my knee,' he said, and suddenly it was there again, the old knowing intimacy in his voice, making her instantly nervous. She took a deep breath and looked at him. Jon Adams. Jon bloody Adams. Dark; long-bodied; a sleepy strong-nosed face; a hidden, telling smile – a 'tall glass of water' – that was what she'd written in her diary. And she'd written so much about him in her diary. He had a quietness about him. If you didn't know, you would say he was reserved, even shy. But she did know, and she knew that what appeared to be shyness was simply the confidence of a man who didn't need to put himself forwards. He was leaning over, rolling up his trouser leg, revealing his strongly muscled calf − that ease he had with his own body. She remembered it too well.

'What did you do to it?' she asked, drawing herself up, straightening her spine, grateful for the white coat and its borrowed authority.

'I tripped down some stairs. I'm working as a waiter at the moment. Hence the outfit,' he said, gesturing to the white shirt and black tie he was wearing. 'I was taking some boxes out the back of the kitchen and misjudged the steps.'

'Do they make you wear an apron with that?' she said, grateful for the chance to tease. 'Those ones that tie round the waist?'

He picked up a white apron from the bed next to him and waved it like a flag of surrender. She smiled, ducked her eyes, stepped towards him. 'I can't imagine you in an apron, Jon.'

'Try harder. You might like it,' he said, and he gave her that half-smile he had always used.

Her hands were on his knee now. It was swollen and she tenderly felt about the joints and tendons, keeping her touch light and inconsequential. But she was suddenly aware of the thigh above the knee and her hands itched to escape from their duty and run all the way up it. His thighs had been miraculous to her, seemingly made of nothing but solid muscle, all firm, nothing like her own softer versions.

'You still run?' she asked, keeping her gaze on his knee, a hot flush creeping over her face.

'I try to,' he said, his quiet voice almost a murmur, 'when I can.'

Crouching before him, she remembered in a rush other times she had knelt before him, and remembered what was now at eye level, in the fold of black at his groin, what she had coveted so much. She had been greedy for it. Too greedy, she thought. Too wanting. Always too eager to take as much as she could in her mouth while he held her head firmly in his hands, his fingers entwined in the rich brown curls of her hair. The suddenness of the memory startled her and she quickly stood upright, tried her best professional smile.

'I think you've just twisted it badly. I'll get a nurse to bind it up and give you some painkillers, you should be fine. Just keep the weight off it for a while. Have a couple of days off work. Come back if it gives you any trouble.'

'OK,' he said, his dark eyes watching her.

She wanted to leave but, just like back at university, something in her wanted to keep his attention for longer. 'So you're a waiter?'

'Training to be a chef,' he said. 'Working my way up. It's that French place by the train station. It's not bad.'

'No, I've heard it's good there. Some friends of mine went recently.' She found herself rocking on her toes, a nervous habit she thought she'd lost.

He smiled, almost sheepishly. 'You've done well,'

he said. 'I always thought you would. You always worked hard. And it suits you.'

'What?'

'The doctor uniform. The white coat. You look good in it. You look like someone people would trust.'

She held his gaze for a moment, aware there was a challenge there, somewhere in what he had said. Inside her, a subversive urge to twist his conventional image of her by saying something filthy rose in her throat.

But she resisted, saying: 'Of course I'm trustworthy, Mr Adams. I have to be. All good doctors are trustworthy. Good luck with the restaurant.' And she turned, quickly, and walked away.

Leaning against a wall in a cubicle in the staff toilet, her breath was rapid. It had always been there between them: this teasing, sexual game of one-upmanship, but she never thought she would see him again after eight years and be so affected by him. Eight years. It was a long time. Yet, pulling up her skirt with her hand and dipping her hand into her knickers, she found a wetness that surprised her. Keeping her hand there, she closed her eyes and remembered how they had met. A party at someone's house. They had ended up sitting on the same sofa. He had made no move towards her, remained leaning back, which she had read as a lack of interest so she merely chatted at him in an increasingly drunken fashion, and it was only after several hours that she noticed that his eyes had never left her face and his leg was pressed against hers in a calm, almost indifferent way. It was a solid, insistent pressure which belied the languor of his upper body, as if he were prepared to take a back seat to his own seduction. And it was that which seduced her: his unobvious attention. She found herself leaning to him and whispering her address – something she never normally did.

'You go on ahead,' he said quietly, as if he had been waiting for her to make her move. 'Leave the door on the latch. When I get there, I want you to be in the bath. You've got ten minutes.'

She had been both vaguely appalled at his presumption – they hadn't even kissed! – yet so excited her thighs were quivering like a nervous racehorse. Despite herself, she rushed home, agonising over whether she should take off her makeup or just hope for the best. Glancing at the clock, she told herself 'Fuck it', ran a bubble bath, quickly stripped and jumped in.

Lying there, in the foamy liquid, she tried to imagine what he – this relative stranger – would want her to do and, feeling oddly self-conscious, she reached between her legs, surprised to find herself already swollen with anticipation. She pressed two fingers to her clit, which immediately responded, sending a judder through her, and she felt a sudden wave of want rise deep inside. And then he was there, filling the doorway of the bathroom, the front door clicking shut in the hall behind him. He said nothing, and his face gave nothing away. He stepped over to where she was lying, blushing pink beneath the bubbles, and he knelt beside her, his thighs endlessly long in blue jeans. He slowly reached out with one hand and encircled her throat, gently but firmly, a caress with a threat, his large hand seeming to surround almost her entire neck, and pulled her towards him, greeting her mouth with a sudden, penetrative tongue, as if to show her what he wanted to do, as if to say: I will take you with this, and then the rest. She felt flooded with heat, returned the kiss, opening her mouth wide, wider, their tongues reaching forwards like they were trying to get further inside than was possible. A sudden hot fucking of tongues. Then he pulled away, the last seconds of his kiss gentle, teasing, and he looked at her, half-smiling.

'Have you washed yourself properly?' he said, almost paternally.

She watched him for a cue then realised she had to improvise to stay in the game, so she grabbed the sponge and held his gaze as she moved it slowly over her breasts, which were standing above the water, two glistening islands. She almost giggled as she sunk her hand below the bubbles and his eyes glimmered briefly with amusement. Rubbing the sponge against herself, she felt her pelvis rise against her hand unconsciously. But it wasn't enough, she wanted to feel her own real wetness, to let him feel her own wetness. She rose, the water falling from her curvaceous body, saying: 'I think I'm clean now.'

Jon's eyes swung up and down her figure, taking in her swaying breasts and rounded hips, her skin shining with liquid. Then he reached for a towel and wrapped her in it, before leaning forwards and picking her up easily to carry her through to the bedroom. Looking down at her as he laid her on the bed, he whispered: 'It's a shame really, because I want to get you really dirty.'

Lying there naked before a man who she had known for only a few hours, Emma knew she could either give into her shyness or go with it, but even before she had conjured up some sexual trick to show him, he had flipped her onto her front and was running his tongue over her buttocks, up and back, then dipping into the slit between them, using his hands to part her, allowing his tongue to circle and then press hotly and insistently into her hole. She screwed her eyes shut, astonished by him, but her eager body had already taken his lead and she was soon arching her back to allow him greater access, spreading herself, rewarding his daring. As she rose, he slid a hand beneath her, a finger slipping each side of her clit, gently moving to and fro as his tongue worked her from behind with the same rhythm. She gasped and pushed back, thrusting at him for more, the pleasure shocking. Then his head moved upwards and he licked his way the whole length of her spine, stopping only to push her hair from the nape of her neck with his free hand so he could bury his mouth in the soft skin behind her ear.

'I want to be inside you,' he told her. The bold simplicity of his statement made her body lurch with lust, and she found herself bucking her naked backside against his groin. She could feel him bulging there, a hard length beneath the denim, and she wanted it. He pulled back momentarily to unbutton his fly and, as she lay there, tremulous, aware of his sticky saliva drying on her skin and her own helpless wetness gathering between her legs, she heard his jeans drop to the ground and felt she had never been more open or more desperate to be open. All shyness was gone. Standing behind her, he used one hand to tilt her body up to him and the other to part her lips to allow him in slowly, achingly slowly, inch by inch, till she felt her whole body was being filled, overtaken. She heard him exhale heavily with pleasure as she met the hilt of his cock and, with one hand on her hip to guide her, he reached forwards to tangle his other hand in the waves of her dark hair, pulling her head back with slow deliberation, so that when she turned her head, he met her to fill her mouth with his hungry tongue. As they moved cock and cunt slowly together, Emma felt as if she was being stretched on some delicious rack, her legs spread wide open to encompass him, her body pulled upwards by the hand gripping her hair. She was abandoned to sensation, shipwrecked on his cock, waves of pleasure rocking her body, soft animal moans coming from her open mouth as she felt the beginning of her climax flutter to life.

But he didn't give her the chance to come. He withdrew and she felt suddenly empty, desperate. She rolled onto her back and, reaching down, grabbed his upright cock and pulled him closer. His half-smile again, and then he took both her hands and held them above her head, able to contain both her wrists in one of his large hands. Pinning her there, he then gently pressed just the tip of himself inside her and teased her like this, seeming to move himself in, then quickly withdrawing, till she had both her feet on the bed, using them as leverage to push her gaping pussy up to meet him. Still he excited her further, using his spare hand to circle her clit with his thumb, tantalising her with his cock, sending concentric waves of sweetness through her, till she felt her vaginal muscles grasp for him like a greedy child's fist and she arched her back and cried out.

'Say it,' he said, slowing the circles of his thumb till his touch was feather-light. 'I want to hear you say it.'

'Fuck me,' she gasped, her voice broken and husky, knowing that was what he wanted to hear, 'please.'

And he did. Standing tall between her legs, he thrust himself fully into her, again and again. The banging of their bodies together, the visceral suction noise of his movement in her wetness, and the repeating spirals of his hand on her clit, worked her upwards and upwards into bliss till she came, dizzyingly hard, her stomach contracting, the pulsations in her pussy jerking her like electric shocks and, seconds later, he came too, pulling out so he could spray himself across her sweat-covered torso, spray-painting her with graffiti, marking her with his fluid, which she found herself rubbing into her flesh dreamily, glad to be coated, lost in her own post-orgasm swoon, not sure who she was, not sure of anything, just fucked – and glad of it.

* * *

And so it had begun. A game where she was never sure of the rules. He would give her instructions and she would comply. Often his commands came at awkward times or when he knew that she would be busy, and she would scrabble to obey, never once failing him. He was never her 'boyfriend'. Her friends never even knew he existed. She knew nothing of his life, though she sometimes told him snippets of her own, when they were lying together afterwards, limbs tangled, and he had stroked her, absent-mindedly, like you would a cat.

And now she was here, in the staff toilet, stroking herself, her clit marble-hard, just thinking of him.

For a week, Emma thought of him. When she was taking the temperature of a child with mumps, she remembered how he would turn up late at night and bend her over the sofa, one hand at her waist, one hand pushing her shoulders down so that her rump was elevated and prone, how they both liked it to be, and how he would fuck her like that, his height lifting her off the ground so she hung on his cock, feet dangling. While she was talking to a woman about her stomach ulcer, she was remembering the night he ordered her to dress like a hooker, and how she had run to a late-night store to get the reddest lipstick she could find so that when he arrived she could take him in her mouth, kneeling obediently in her fishnet stockings, leaving red smears like paint along the length of him, feeling the head of his cock pushing against the back of her throat as she stayed open for him, saliva dripping from her straining mouth. As she treated a complex elbow fracture, she thought of the night he had decreed silence, how they had met in the darkness of her bed (never his) and touched each other like the blind, fingers tracing faces, sketching bodies, and how he pushed two fingers into her soft, warm mouth and she sucked hungrily till he took two more fingers, licked them himself, and wriggled them gently inside her tight arsehole till her pussy sprang to life, jealous, until he filled that too with the smooth satisfaction of his cock, and she rocked on him, drunk with feeling, all entrances filled – mouth, cunt, arse – all stretched, all used, nothing left.

While she filled in prescription forms, she remembered how he had ordered her to meet him at a hotel bar pretending to be a lonely stranger, how she had played the part of a troubled wife, even twirling a second-hand ring on her wedding finger, till he took her to the lift and made her face the wall, her hands held down by his on the cold metal of the wall, while her lifted her skirt and took her rapidly from behind, hard and animal, till her knees buckled as she felt him come inside her in sharp, sudden jerks. And when the man she was casually dating tried to persuade her to go on top because he thought it was adventurous, she imagined she was with Jon, who liked her lying face down, mouth in the pillow, with his whole body covering her, slamming himself into her as their bodies slapped together like percussion and with each thrust she was somewhere further away, further gone, almost unconscious, unable to remember who or where she was till he whispered in her ear that he loved fucking her, he loved fucking her, Emma.

These games they had played. A contest of power and submission. And even at this latest meeting, somehow he still had the advantage. Yet eight years had passed. Surely he couldn't be allowed the upper hand any more. She had stockings somewhere didn't she? Somewhere in the wardrobe were high fuck-me heels. And she had a white coat. She had a uniform. She would be let in anywhere.

His uniform, by contrast, made him anonymous. As she watched through the window of the restaurant, she saw how the diners failed to even recognise him as a person: he was just one of many in a white shirt and a black tie. He merely brought them food, filled their glasses, moved their chairs. Strangely, it excited her, seeing him in a position of subservience: it made her new purpose seem clearer, despite the fact it was a cold night, and she was wearing nothing but stockings, heels, a stethoscope and a white coat beneath her short belted mac. She grasped her doctor's bag for reassurance, it was like a talisman to her, part of the costume. It also contained her mobile phone, which she glanced at, saw four messages from the man she was avoiding, and switched it off. She didn't know yet what she was doing, but she didn't need any distraction.

It took all her courage to push open the restaurant door and stride towards the maître'd, who eyed her curious outfit with distaste. She gave him her best worried doctor face.

'I apologise for the intrusion – I've come straight from the hospital,' she said, the words falling magically from her mouth even as her brain skittered in panic. 'I saw a member of your staff earlier this week and I'm afraid one of our junior doctors completely misread his X-ray and this man – Jon Adams is his name – shouldn't be working at all. I'm here because … well, basically it's my responsibility – the junior is under my charge – and if this man damages his knee by walking on it when he shouldn't, it will be my fault.'

The maître'd dropped his air of superciliousness and gestured to another waiter to fetch Jon.

Emma continued: 'I do apologise for interrupting your evening like this, but he needs to come back to the hospital.' She could feel the eyes of the restaurant customers on her, felt the respectful hush of people who had seen a doctor enter the room. The power of her position filled her with confidence like a straight shot of vodka.

And suddenly, Jon was there, standing in front of her, looking down on her, mild confusion knitting his brow. She looked him straight in the eye. 'Ah, Mr Adams, if you'd like to come with me.' She gestured to the door.

Jon's eyes flickered, trying to read her, then he took off his apron and handed it to his colleague. 'Of course,' he said, his voice oddly hesitant. But he followed her out.

'I have a car,' she said over her shoulder, as she

strode down the pavement on her precarious heels. She reached it and opened the passenger door for him. 'Get in,' she said. He did.

She drove him to her flat, saying nothing, letting him wonder. The night road passed beneath them, the small blue lights on the dashboard glowed. Once, he opened his mouth as if to speak but said nothing. She felt the naked skin of her arse resting against the cool cotton of her white coat and tensed her inner muscles with gleeful anticipation, flashing him a reassuring doctor's smile as she swung the car expertly up her drive.

He followed her inside as she walked ahead of him, hitting all the light switches till the whole apartment was bathed and glowing, and then she stood in the centre of her living room, hands on hips.

'What's this about?' he began, but she pressed a finger to her lips, feeling like an actress in a film as she unbelted her mac. It could all go wrong, she thought, but she would give it a shot.

Standing before him in her white coat, she said: 'I'm your doctor. And I want to physically examine you.'

'Emma, you –'

She silenced him with a sharp tilt of her head. 'It's Dr Cooper to you. And first, you should bring me a drink ... waiter,' she said, and she let her gaze idle up and down his demeaning restaurant uniform.

Jon opened his mouth slowly, his eyebrows raised. She held her ground. She knew – or at least, she hoped she knew – that he couldn't resist a dare.

The silence hung between them. She could hear her own breath.

'Gin and tonic?' he said. His voice was strangely meek.

'Ice and a slice,' she replied, nodding to the kitchen.

By the time he had returned bearing her drink she had undone the top buttons of her coat, revealing the skin between her breasts down to just above her belly button. She accepted the drink and took a gulp, savouring the bitter cool liquid in her throat, before saying: 'Undress.'

'What?'

'I said undress.'

Again his eyes flickered, but he was intrigued now. He stared at her, appreciatively, admiring the contrast between her sensible white coat and the exposed flesh it revealed, as he undid his tie and slowly took off his shirt. She inhaled deeply at the sight of his chest, the line of dark hairs that ran down from mid-chest past his navel to his groin like a road map. He paused then, half-naked, but she raised an eyebrow and that was enough. Obediently, he unbuckled his belt, took off his trousers, shoes and socks and stood before her in his boxer shorts, which, she noted approvingly, were straining at the fly.

'Those too,' she said.

His half-smile was rueful but he complied, pulling his boxers off, and he presented himself for her, stripped, his erection quivering slightly as it stood up before him. She eyed him from a professional distance and took another slug of her drink, keeping an ice cube in her mouth. Then, in a slow casual movement, she stepped forwards, bending from the waist and took his cock between her lips, running her tongue along the underside, letting the ice cube run with her. Jon gasped and shuddered, clasped her head, but Emma shook him off and after one quick up–down stroke, let him go, stood upright and spat the ice cube back into her glass.

'I want you to kneel, Mr Adams,' she said, becoming more aware of the nagging between her legs. He did as he was told, his lengthy cock bouncing almost comically. She set down her drink and slowly unbuttoned her white coat all the way down, revealing a long bare strip of her body, from collarbone to stomach to the neat strip of her pubic hair to the ripe flesh that bulged over her black stocking tops. Emma moved away from him slowly until she could lean back against her living room wall, and then she spread her legs to reveal herself, stepping out of first one high heel, then the other, then tipping her pelvis out and reaching down to part herself for him with the fingers of one hand. With her other hand, she reached up to hold onto the stethoscope that hung round her neck. 'I want you to stick out your tongue,' she said, 'and say "ah".'

A brief smirk passed across Jon's face as he shuffled forwards on his knees. Eagerly he grasped a stockinged thigh in each hand and pulled her towards him as his face buried itself between her legs. His tongue delved immediately inside her – like a substitute cock, he pushed it in repeatedly until she grabbed hold of his hair and slowly pulled him a few inches higher.

'Start here, please, Mr Adams,' she said, moving his mouth to her clit. 'I'll monitor your results and tell you when you're done. Doctor's orders.'

As his hot tongue lapped at her, Emma felt her legs weaken. She tipped her head back, gripped the stethoscope harder, her nails digging into the flesh of her palm. He was eager, rushing almost. It was like he wanted to consume her. He opened his mouth wide, taking all of her in, sucking and licking, groaning with muffled pleasure. His hands let go of her legs to join him at the front, his fingers gently pulling her lips apart to open her and allow him to suck her swollen clit like a nipple, then slowly sliding a single finger inside her to make her aware of her slippery inner passage and its delicious ache to be filled.

Emma roused herself. Pulled herself up. 'I want you to lie down over there, Mr Adams,' she said gesturing through the living-room door to the table in the kitchen, aware that her authoritative gaze had melted somewhat, her eyes muddied and unfocused. He did as he was told, lay his long muscled body down and stretched out under the lights, as if he were on an operating table.

As Emma pulled up a chair so she could get up on the table and straddle him, she caught sight of her reflection in the kitchen window, her white coat flowing out behind her semi-naked body like a cape, her full breasts bobbing as she moved, the tendons in her thighs visible as she swung her leg across him, her eyes dark and giving away nothing.

I'd like to fuck you, she thought, watching as she lowered herself till she hung just above him.

She turned to him, fearless now: 'I'd like you to fuck me, Mr Adams, would you?'

He smiled, fully this time, no half-measures. 'Dr Cooper, I'd like to fuck you very much.'

Emma knelt on the wooden table above him, her wetness just inches away from his upright cock. His eyes were fixed on her. She sat back on her haunches and took him in her hands, then moved forwards to rub herself against him. She pressed his cock against her so it pushed up along her clit and parted her lips, coating him in her juice, then she moved him back down and did it again.

'Emma, let me −'

'Shh. I'm concentrating.'

She was busy now, a doctor at work, a sexual surgeon, involved only in her own gratification, that urgent clitoral buzzing that required her to pull him up and down against her, there was nothing else like it, she thought as she threw her head back, and right now, he was her masturbatory tool.

But the more she did it, the more she wanted that solid, straining piece of flesh inside her. She wanted to feel his length knocking against her cervix, pushing her body over the edge. So, looking down at him, she pulled off her white coat, leaving herself bare but for her stockings under the neon kitchen lights and she positioned herself so that she was teetering on the end of his cock and she stayed there, while he writhed beneath her, for as long as she could before eventually sinking down on him, enveloping him exquisitely, both of them gasping with release. Then, as she slowly circled her pelvis on top of him, she reached forwards and placed his hands over his head, holding him down with one hand, using the other to take the stethoscope from around her neck so she could tie his wrists with it. Then, when he was bound, she leaned down slowly, letting her breasts graze his chest, to place one hand around his throat, a caress with a threat, gave him a familiar half-smile, and opened his mouth with hers so she could fuck him, again and again, with her efficient doctor's tongue.

Afterwards, she sat on the edge of her kitchen table, feeling pleasantly groggy, sleepily sated, swinging her legs to and fro, perusing the rips in her stockings. Jon pulled on his regulation black trousers and watched her.

'So,' he said, zipping himself back in.

'So,' she replied, and paused to push her tangled hair back from her eyes so she could look at him equally.

'Do you think I'll need another examination?' he said.

'Wait to hear from me,' she said. 'I'll be reviewing your case.'

'Yes, Doctor,' he replied, picking up his shirt, adding: 'Although, I may have to contact you at some point, if there's an emergency, for example, late at night. You never know, these things happen.'

Emma smiled and gently sucked on her own bottom lip for a moment, tasting him there, the salt of his sweat, the sweet earthiness of his cock. 'We'll both just have to wait and see, then, won't we?'

Jessica Donnolly's short stories have appeared in the Wicked Words collections *Sex in the Kitchen* and *Sex in Uniform*.

Pumps Monica Belle

I have a confession to make. There's a naughty habit I picked up in college, or maybe I should say a nasty habit. Yes, a nasty habit, as the Americans put it, because it's something that respectable women very definitely do not do – but it is delightfully sexy.

The first time was at the beginning of my second year. I'd bought an ancient Metro, my first ever car, to get my stuff up to college. It was nearly two hundred miles, so I decided to fill my tank right up and make sure I didn't run out of petrol. After buying the car I had to watch every penny, so I went to the supermarket pumps the night before I left. It was two in the morning and nobody was about except for a bored attendant reading a magazine in his booth. I'd parked a bit too close to the pumps, and when I put the nozzle in the hose pressed to my leg, just a couple of inches from the V of my jeans, so that when I squeezed the trigger . . .

I had never realised a petrol pump vibrated like that, so fast, and so powerful, the thick green hose sending shivers right through me, and right where it matters. Of course I snatched it away immediately, sure I'd been seen, but there was nobody there to see me, and that single jolt of pleasure had been far too good to ignore. My car was between me and the booth, and it was more than I could resist not to push the hose against me again, this time right between my thighs, with the trigger squeezed full on.

It made me feel guilty, and slightly silly, but it made me feel daring too, while those vibrations were far, far too good to let me stop. I had to close my eyes, the feeling was so strong, jolting me into a sudden arousal far more quickly than anything I'd known before, and made stronger still by my sense of being naughty and my fear of getting caught. All anybody needed to do was drive up behind me and they'd see, see what I was doing with the thick green hose between my legs, see how improper I was being, masturbating in public, how naughty, how dirty.

I squeezed my thighs tighter, biting my lip in a vain effort to stop the pleasure showing on my face as it rose higher and higher still. A little more and I was going to come, right there on the garage forecourt, to come in public. How bad could I get? I was masturbating in public. I was going to come in public. I was . . .

. . . not going to do anything of the sort, because the tank was full and the automatic cut-off had worked perfectly for once, leaving the hose still thick and firm between my thighs, but not vibrating. I had never, ever felt so frustrated, and, short of rubbing myself on the hose, which was far too blatant, there was nothing I could do. My hands were shaking, and the sense of urgency between my thighs was every bit as high as it had ever been before, even during those exquisite moments an instant before penetration, when you know your lover's cock is going to go in at the next instant.

I was so aroused I even considered propositioning the attendant, something completely outside my experience. He wasn't very attractive, or maybe I would have done, although I doubt it. I'd have lost my nerve, anyway, back then, after just three lovers and all of them very conventional – rather like me really, until then.

There was nothing conventional about what I did when I got home. I desperately needed to recreate my experience as soon as possible. Everyone else was asleep, my room quiet and almost dark, with just the dull orange glow of the street light outside to illuminate me as I stood by my bed, stroking myself through my jeans and struggling to focus my mind on what I'd done.

It wasn't easy. I needed to be clothed and I needed to be standing, but I also needed something thick and rubbery between my thighs, something that vibrated. There wasn't anything. Even if I'd had a boyfriend to hand he'd have needed at least three feet of impressively thick, vibrating cock, and they just don't make men like that. I was going to do it, though, one way or another, and in the end I nipped downstairs to fetch a bottle of salad dressing from the fridge.

I held it between my thighs as I rubbed myself on it, thinking of how rude it had felt to secretly masturbate in public. It did feel good, and naughty, and it got me there in the end, but the thrill was very pale indeed compared with the real thing.

Even as I came down from the peak of my excitement I knew I'd be doing it again.

The trouble was, that no matter what, the petrol tank of my Metro was simply not big enough to take me all the way. I tried again and again, all that year and always to much the same routine. Half my money went on petrol, and I was the most popular girl in my hall because I was always willing to give lifts, help people move their things and generally put my car to use whenever I possibly could.

As soon as my tank was empty I'd stay up late, then drive out to one of the big, anonymous petrol stations on the ring road. Sometimes I'd be unlucky and there would be too many people about, but more often than not it would be OK and I would get my moment of mounting ecstasy before driving home to bring myself to climax under sticky fingers.

I soon became something of an expert. For instance, it's always best to go to the right-hand pump, because then there's the best chance of being shielded from the prying eyes of both the attendant and fellow motorists. Unless, of course, your petrol tank is on the left, in which case the reverse is true. Always wear dark clothes, because believe me, walking into a student accommodation block in white jeans with the outline of your sex lips set off with oily black lowlights takes quite a bit of explaining.

Otherwise jeans are good, because nobody comments if you wear them tight, but if I get too excited I make a damp patch, which can be awkward. Slacks are more embarrassing still, because the damp patch shows more easily, but they let the vibrations right through, especially with no knickers on underneath. Skirts are awkward, unless you dare to lift them up, but I'm getting ahead of myself.

All that year it was the same, and most of the next. I did feel guilty about it, sometimes, and that it somehow made me abnormal, but then I'd tell myself it was just harmless fun. Twice I gave it up, once during a brief fling with a fellow student, a law graduate who'd already been through Yale. He was nice, and maybe I even loved him a little, but I knew I could never share my nasty little secret with him and stopped it until we split up. The day after I'd dumped him I was back at the pumps.

The second time was during finals, when I swore I'd stop because it was spoiling my concentration on my work. I succeeded too, although as the days ticked by I could feel my need rising, and while all my fellow students were getting outrageously drunk at our party after the final exam I was on orange juice, the designated driver, which allowed me to visit my favourite service station at four o'clock in the morning.

I graduated with a 2:1 and took up a PhD grant even further from home than before. Most of my friends were going into work, which meant salaries, and it took me quite a bit of willpower not to do the same. Not because I wanted to join the ranks of the wage slaves, you understand, but because it would have meant I could afford a bigger car. A bigger car meant more petrol. More petrol meant more time to fill up. More time to fill up might just mean that I could bring my nasty little habit to the climax that had eluded me for so long.

Being a good girl at heart, I resisted, but it was only when I'd settled down in the north of England to work on my thesis that I discovered the joys of demonstrating. I'd been vaguely aware that graduates could add to their pay by taking practicals, but I'd never realised how well it paid, or how much was available. To the delight of my tutors I took on work in every subject I could handle, and quite a few I wasn't at all sure about.

For the first time in my life I was earning money, and I knew exactly what I wanted to buy. Well, not exactly, because it took me a while to work out which of the models I could afford would take the longest to fill up. I shall skip over the details, save to say that the most fanatic anorak would have been amazed at me as I sat up over my calculations, surrounded by car catalogues new and old, drinking coffee after coffee until I was satisfied.

At last I made my selection, a big old Ford with a fifteen-gallon tank, twice as big as the one in my Metro. I know it sounds silly, and the sort of thing only men are supposed to do, but as I drove away from the dealer's forecourt I felt as if I were going on a first date, and felt bad about 'dumping' my Metro. As usual, feeling a bit silly didn't stop me, and, as there was almost nothing in the tank, I knew it wouldn't be long.

I drove myself home and forced myself to take

my time over dinner, then sit down and watch TV for a bit, although my hands kept straying either to my car keys or to the V between my thighs. Only at midnight did I allow myself to go into my bedroom, take off the skirt and knickers I'd worn during the day and slip into tight, slimline black slacks with nothing underneath. One glance in the mirror was enough to be sure it showed, with my bottom cheeks bare and round underneath the thin cotton, and the shape of my sex embarrassingly obvious at the front.

Anyone who saw me would know I had no panties, which made me hesitate, but after half an hour of indecision I told myself to be bold, and out I went. It was still a little early, but I drove out of town, to a big service station beside the road leading up over the Pennines. I knew it was never very busy in the evening, and sure enough, as I pulled in, only one other car was there, a souped-up cabriolet driven by overexcited teenagers.

They seemed to take forever, laughing among themselves and going back and forth from the booth to fetch cigarettes and chocolates, until I was cursing them under my breath. All the while I'd been pretending to have trouble with my petrol cap, and praying nobody would offer to help me. They didn't, and as soon as the other car had roared off I twisted it open, only to discover that the attendant was looking right at me.

I knew why, or I thought I did. The teenagers had been in my favourite spot and he could see me, with the light full on me from behind. His eyes were right on me, and, although I dared not turn around, I could just imagine them lingering on the contours of my bottom, so obviously bare beneath my slacks. I didn't know what to do, too embarrassed to simply drive away, while indulging my nasty habit with him watching was absolutely out of the question.

In the end I put in a miserable two pounds' worth of petrol and endured both the funny look he gave me when I paid and the feel of his eyes on my bottom as I walked back to my car. I was blushing as I drove away, with my hands shaking on the wheel, but I was determined not to give in. There was another service station a couple of miles south on the main trunk road, bigger and busier, but maybe I'd be lucky.

I was. A large van had pulled into the second pump from the right, allowing me to take the perfect place and shielding me from the attendant. My heart was racing as I slipped the nozzle from its holster and into the mouth of my petrol tank, and faster still as I surreptitiously closed my thighs around the thick, rubbery hose. Ready, I made myself wait, just a second, and squeezed.

As the vibrations hit me I felt my mouth become wide in pleasure, and shut it just in time to prevent myself getting caught as the van driver appeared around the front of his vehicle. That gave me a start, but he took no notice of me whatsoever, and as he pulled out my pleasure was already rising towards ecstasy. I was going to do it, I really was, to make myself come with a petrol hose, after so long. That was enough, no fantasy needed, just the way I was, knickerless under my slacks, the hose pumping between my tightly clenched thighs, the vibrations running through my sex, masturbating in public, as usual, but this time to orgasm, my pleasure rising, my muscles beginning to tighten, my bottom squeezing, my eyes closed in bliss, delicious little shocks starting in my pussy . . .

. . . and nothing, as the pump cut out, just seconds before ecstasy overwhelmed me. My eyes came open and I looked down, the thick green hose between my thighs blurred, my legs weak with the approach of orgasm, my hands shaking so hard I could barely put the pump back and twist the petrol cap into place. I paid. I drove away. I stopped, in a lay-by just a few hundred yards down the road, because I quite simply was not fit to drive.

I'd been so close, right on the edge of orgasm, yet I had been denied that final push to take me over the brink. Maybe, just maybe, I'd have made it if the van driver hadn't appeared. Maybe, just maybe, I'd have made it if I hadn't put two pounds' worth in already. It would work, another time, that I knew, but it was no help. I couldn't wait, my frustration too strong to be denied.

Still trembling badly, I wound my seat back a little. Just yards outside my window cars were belting past, and yet I couldn't stop myself. My legs became wide, my hand pressed to the V of my crotch, and I was masturbating, not even subtly, but sighing as I rubbed myself through my slacks, alternately squeezing and spreading my thighs, my eyes shut, one hand to my breasts to tease and stroke my nipples, my mouth wide in pleasure, and then in ecstasy as I brought myself to a shuddering, wriggling climax that left me with spots dancing in front of my eyes and my head spinning and dizzy.

That was the first time I had ever come outdoors, at least alone, which is very different from being in the arms of a lover. Afterwards I was telling myself that it had been a stupid thing to do, especially right beside the main road, and that I would never do it again. You see, the great thing about the petrol pump was that it looked quite innocent, except only that last crucial moment, and I'd spent ages teaching myself to look as unflustered as possible as I came. In the lay-by I'd looked anything but innocent, with my legs wide open and playing with my breasts as I rubbed myself. If a patrol car had happened to pull in at the wrong moment to see what the matter was I'd have been in serious trouble. Or it might have been a lorry driver, or a group of teenage tearaways out for fun, like the ones I'd seen earlier.

I knew I'd be back, but I promised myself I'd be more careful. I was, and I wasn't. The next occasion came quite unexpectedly, when I was asked to drive the departmental minibus to take some students down to York. I agreed to do it, and was telling myself I would be good as I drew in to the very same service station at which I'd come so close before. It was impossible to be good. Just taking the pump in my hand sent a shiver the length of my spine, and watching the way the hose moved had me squeezing my thighs together.

None of the students were looking as I stood

behind the van, blocked from sight. It was too much for me. Full of apprehension and guilty excitement, I moved a little closer, allowing the thickness of the hose to press into my sex as I squeezed the trigger home. I was in heaven immediately, but, with the need to keep a straight face and my concern for the students and others using the garage, I knew I would never reach that magic moment. Sure enough, I didn't, but I rode my ecstasy for the full time it took me to fill up that big, big tank, which left me dizzy with pleasure and need.

Naturally, I couldn't do what I wanted to in front of my students, so I was left smouldering gently for the rest of the day. Only that evening did I manage to come, and, as I lay in the warm stillness of my bedroom afterwards, my head was full of plans for that ultimate moment of satisfaction. With my car I might make it, but with the minibus I would *definitely* make it, while it also provided so much more shelter. All I needed to do was find some excuse to book it out for the day, on a trip long enough to make sure I came back late at night and so could replace the petrol I'd used in my own special way.

Which I did. My trip took me up into the Highlands, a beautiful drive, with my sense of anticipation rising all day, until, by the time I was ready to start back, I could barely contain myself. I'd planned which petrol station to use, but I never made it that far. With the tank just on the red I came across an empty station on an empty road, and I took my opportunity.

It was perfect. The attendant was dozing in his booth and there was nobody else around. Now I was going to do it, and just that knowledge was enough to have me shaking as I unlocked the petrol cap, full of guilt and arousal, knowing that this time there was no stopping, no going back. I slid out the pump from its holster and pushed the nozzle deep. I pressed close to the hose, pushing the thick, hard rubber tight against the crotch of my favourite black slacks, beneath which I had no knickers. I squeezed the trigger and closed my eyes, knowing exactly what was going to happen.

The moment the vibrations started to run through my sex I knew I was there. I felt such a bad girl, so deliciously rude. Everyone at the university thought I was such a good girl, ever so diligent, always ready to help, working hard, far too shy and far too serious to even think about men. The last bit was true, anyway. Who needs men? I didn't, not with a two-inch-thick rubber hose pumping petrol between my thighs.

It was going to happen, my excitement rising, my thighs tight around the hose, my head full of naughty thoughts, and I was there, biting my lip to stop myself crying out as wave after wonderful wave of pure bliss swept over me, on and on until my knees gave way and I was forced to stop. I sank down, leaning against the side of the minibus, my head spinning with reaction to what I'd done, my hand still grasping the trigger, pumping petrol.

I became an addict. There's no other word for it. Again and again I would go out, with my car, with the minibus, even with friends' cars once or twice, to run through that same delightful routine: a quiet service station, the hose between my thighs, the trigger squeezed, and taken to heaven by the vibrations.

I was always very careful to keep my nasty little habit a secret, but the more I did it the more I needed it, and the more I did it the less exciting it became each time. I understood full well the path I was on, and I did my best to restrict myself to doing it once a week and to resist the urges of my imagination, which was demanding that I try new and more exciting routines, more exciting, and more daring. I tried to resist, but I failed.

The first temptation I gave in to was to do it with the hose pressed to the front of my knickers, a small thing maybe, but not when it means standing on the forecourt of a petrol station with my skirt bunched up at the front so that I could press the hose to myself. I'd been thinking about it for a while, and how easy it would be in a knee-length skirt. And it was. It was also delightful, with the feel of my bare thighs and the knowledge of how unmistakably rude I would look restoring all the pleasure I'd lost through overfamiliarity. That was one cool summer dawn beside a road in Wales, and it was the first of many times.

The second temptation I gave in to was the urge to feel the touch of the hose on my bare flesh. That was at a petrol station outside Rugby, the first time, when the thrill of pressing the hose to the front of my knickers had begun to fade. I reasoned that, if I dared to push up the front of my skirt to get at my knickers, then why not do it with no knickers underneath? After all, I wouldn't be showing anything else. But I was, flashing my bare sex for just an instant as I adjusted myself, and that made it better still, giving me one of the best orgasms I'd ever had. Once I'd done it bare, there was no going back.

The third temptation I gave in to was to let somebody else see. I'd fought it hard, for two long years, scared by the power of my own needs as much as by the possible consequences of my action. By then I'd taken to doing bare every time, and as often as not after a little routine. I would choose my time and choose my place, then drive out late at night as always. I would be dressed in a sensible, knee-length skirt, stay-up stockings and no knickers. Just being bare was wonderful, and sometimes I would even stop just to take my knickers off under my skirt, even when it wasn't a petrol day.

That was what I did on the day it happened. I was travelling from London to Carlisle in my shiny new BMW, a treat I'd bought myself on getting my new job as a senior researcher with my company. For some reason I was feeling aroused anyway, and as I watched the petrol gauge drop slowly down I decided to tease myself. After pulling off at the next services, I parked in the far corner and slipped off my knickers under my skirt. I had lunch there, enjoying the naughty feeling of having my bare bottom sitting on the chair and knowing that I was bare.

By the time I left the services I was ready, and I stayed ready as I drove north, all the time imagining the pleasure of the climax I was going to give myself that evening when I filled up the car. Had I stayed on the motorway I'd have been in Carlisle far too early, so I turned off beyond Lancaster and threaded my way north through the Lake District. For dinner, I ate at country pub, again with my bottom bare on the seat beneath me, and, not long after I left, the warning for low fuel came on.

For me, that was like a switch. With some women it might be the sight of their favourite film star, for others a pair of muscular buttocks packed into tight jeans. For me, it is the moment that little yellow light comes on and I know that it is time to masturbate. Now was no exception, even though it was a little early. I pulled off the road just a few miles later, at a tiny station high on a hillside. It looked as if it hadn't changed since the 70s, just two pumps, side by side, with no canopy, and a wooden stack in which the attendant was seated, resting the plaster cast that encased a broken leg on a chair. The thought came to me immediately. He could see me. He could hardly fail to see me, but I was quite safe. After all, what was he going to do?

What he was going to do was enjoy the view. I knew he was right immediately I went to the booth to buy a packet of mints. He was young, handsome, friendly in an easygoing way, and yet as I walked back to the car his eyes were on my bottom, watching the way my bare cheeks moved under my skirt. He knew I was bare, I was sure of it, and that alone was a delicious thrill.

Turning to find him smiling at me was more delicious still, and, with my heart in my throat, I decided to do it. I waved, making it quite clear I knew he was watching. I opened my petrol cap and took the pump from the holster, as I had done so often before, but now knowing a man was watching, and my sense of rising anticipation was stronger even than it had been those first few times.

Had I not been so turned on I could never have done it, but I was, and I did. I made sure he was watching. I took hold of the front of my dress. I lifted it, deliberately showing my legs, my stocking tops, my bare thighs and my bare sex, naked and pink in the fluorescent light, bare to his pop-eyed gaze.

That alone was enough to leave me determined to make myself come. I was shaking terribly, but I took the pump and eased it between my legs, showing off with a little wriggle as I made myself comfortable with the hose pressed deep into the groove of my sex. I kept my skirt up, too, so that he could see, every rude detail as I began to do it, squeezing the trigger and rubbing myself on the hose as that wonderful, throbbing vibration began.

Now he was really staring, with his mouth open wide, and that only encouraged me. I began to let my feelings show on my face, maybe even putting it on a little as I wriggled and squirmed against the hose. There was nothing fake about my pleasure, though, my orgasm already rising in my head as I thought of what I was doing: not just masturbating in public, but doing it bare, and in front of a man.

I came, screaming out my pleasure as it hit me, with the hose pumping hard between my thighs, my whole body tight with ecstasy, my sex on fire. He was staring as hard as ever, and, as that glorious orgasm tore through, I locked eyes with him, watching him as he watched me come, holding his gaze until at last I could take it no more and slumped down, spent.

Only then did I realise that I hadn't really thought it through, letting myself get carried away in my excitement. What I'd meant to do was come, then cover myself up, perhaps give him a final teasing wave, and leave. Unfortunately it was out of the question.

I'd come in front of him, and my tank was full of petrol, petrol I hadn't paid for. Forty-two pounds and thirty-eight pence the pump showed, forty-two pounds and thirty-eight pence I was going to have to pay him. That meant walking across the forecourt, handing my debit card to the man I had just masturbated in front of, waiting for him to put it through his machine, signing for the payment and walking back to the car.

Never, ever have I been so embarrassed, my face burning with blushes as I walked, acutely aware not only of what I'd done, but of how I was, and how he knew I was, bare under my skirt. I wondered if he'd say something, maybe call me a slut or a tease, maybe demand that I lift my skirt again and show off for him. He just smiled, which is why he is now my husband, and tonight he is taking me out, to this little petrol station I know just a few miles up the A32.

Monica Belle is the author of the Black Lace novels *Nobel Vices*, *Valentina's Rules*, *Wild by Nature*, *Office Perks*, *Pagan Heat*, *Bound in Blue* and *The Boss*. Her short stories have appeared in numerous Wicked Words collections.

Lovely Cricket Jan Bolton

It was Dad who started it off. I blame him. He was the one who badgered me into signing up for the Rothermere Eleven. I told him I wasn't interested in cricket – or bloody football or hockey – but he never listened to me. I'd been dragged – well, driven – protesting to the practice nets twice a week and, even though I never seemed to be putting that much effort into it, I cultivated a medium-pace spin technique that Dad said reminded him of Daniel Vittori's. I'm long in the leg and I soon perfected the timing of letting the ball free from my grasp, making sure it carried full momentum behind it. By the time the batsman had realised he'd underestimated me, the bails were already on the ground. I'm no slouch at the crease, either. I hit fours every game, much to everyone's surprise, not least my own and bounded down the wicket in fewer strides than it took most of my opponents. By mid-March I was in the elite squad. Me – Chris Cavendish. I could barely believe it.

The upper and lower sixth cricket tournament happens every June, when we play the equivalent teams from Sir William Levington. It's a school tradition – part of sports week. All the old crocks get wheeled up there for the day in their MCC and old school ties, straw trilbies and cravats and blazers. There's always a reception afterwards in the long room opposite the pavillion and, if it's a hot day, drinks are served by the lower years on the perimeter lawn. It's all very English and polite.

Dad was overjoyed when I made the upper eleven. He kept going on about having my name on that cup, like his had been thirty years back. The photo has been up in his study since I can remember – him and his hairy classmates back in the mid seventies, proud jaws and great prospects, prog rock on vinyl in the evening and Brian Johnston on long wave in the afternoon.

It's a bit late now to say it would never have happened if I hadn't been in the team. But how was I to know that the sight of me in my whites would be the final spark that would ignite the Roman candle of emotions in Melinda Parry – mother of my classmate Jason and the owner of the finest pair of tits in the borough, the South East, the country – to fizz and combust in a torrent of brief but beautiful flames.

As I sit here now, in my bedroom, waiting for the fallout, I try to tell myself I don't really give that much of a toss about it, 'cos I'm off to university in September, and they'll have forgotten about it by Christmas. I hope. But I don't think I can rely on that little nest-egg Dad promised me a couple of months back. The sight of his face when he caught us was something I'll never forget. And now I've been grounded pending a serious chat when he gets back here in about an hour.

I still can't believe it happened. It felt so right but, of course, I realise now that it was very, very wrong. I should have talked about it with someone, but it's not something you chat about with your parents, is it? How would it go? 'All right, ma, I've got the raging horn for my best mate's mum. Leave us alone for a bit, will you.' No, it just wouldn't be right.

I guess that's the thing about suburban life ... no one dares speak about sex but it occupies a large amount of the residents' daily thoughts – the not getting it, that is. It's the not getting it that landed me in hot water. Whatever happens I'm not going to blame her for seducing me, which she did, kind of, but it was hardly rape of a minor. I mean, it wasn't illegal – just immoral. I've never been one for false modesty and 'Oh, I shouldn'ts'. I always hated hearing my female relatives say that at birthdays and Christmas whenever Mum had wrapped up some cheapo toiletries to give out to them, supposedly from me. 'Oh, you shouldn't have!' they'd trill. Well I'm not going to say that, 'cos I did, and I have no regrets. And I'd do it all over again. If I could ...

Jason's mum stopped me dead in my tracks the first time I met her – nearly three years back. I was besotted, but I kept it well hidden. I don't think Jase suspected anything. He was usually head down in one of his snowboarding magazines or playing Grand Theft Auto. I'd never been that bothered about gaming before, but once I'd clocked Jason's mum I cultivated an interest that had me round their place all hours after school. I was happy to smack up some CGI pimps if it meant I could see Melinda. I'd be invited to tea, and to Sunday lunch sometimes.

Jason's parents were divorced. His dad was the competitive type, the opposite temperament to Jason and his mum. I guessed that Melinda liked that kind of powerful man who would lavish her with fine things – jewellery and fancy holidays and perfume and knickers. But I was wrong about that. I distinctly remember staring into a fruits of the forest Pavlova and drifting off to thinking what I could give her as a little present and thinking I didn't have a chance of impressing her. And then I realised I had turned into a romantic fool. Early on in my visits I bought her a bunch of flowers – for having me round to tea so often – and I went purple with embarrassment when she leant in to kiss me thanks. But the touch of her hand on my shoulder sent me into paroxysms of delight and I shivered under the warmth of it.

I recall being in the Parrys' garden, at dusk, late last year – just me and Melinda, sitting on the padded sun swing, gently rocking back and forth. Jason was having his Sunday bath and I was acutely aware of being alone with Melinda, who had her neat, tanned bare legs curled under her. I couldn't help my eyes from darting to where her dress had been pushed up. I was ten centimetres from luscious female thigh flesh and I was in pain from wanting to touch her. By this time I was besotted with her, and there was no stopping the tide. We were talking about the future; about my studies and what universities I was applying for, but all I wanted to talk about was how lovely I thought she looked. I must have been sounding less than confident because – and I remember it as if it were yesterday – she brushed her hand through my thick blonde hair and told me everything would be fine.

At that moment I wanted to fall upon her; to kiss her deeply and rip the light cotton dress from her shoulders and roll her down on to the grass. I wanted to be a beast with her and offer her my virginity and tell her she was beautiful. Her hair was shining in the early evening light and she looked so tempting – I sensed a wealth of erotic treasures could be mine, if only I could make the right connection. She was a woman in the prime of her life and she needed to be worshipped. I didn't have experience, and that was obviously what she would want from a lover, but I had plenty of enthusiasm. If only I had known then what she was like – that she too had strong desires, especially for younger men – I may well have acted upon my lusts a lot earlier. But I gritted my teeth and smiled thinly and pressed my hands between my knees in discomfort and shame at having my hair tousled by my mate's mum. There I was, thinking that she saw me as 'sweet' or something, and all the time she was planning on taking things a lot further.

Humans are cursed by shyness. Where does it come from? Why is it the most difficult thing in the world to tell someone you fancy them? I don't understand why it causes so much fuss. Unless a person is obviously displaying signs of arousal – and, personally, I find it very difficult to tell if a woman is aroused – potential couples can go through their lives never taking that essential chance that can make all the difference to one's sexual history. And that kills me.

A year makes a lot of difference when you're my age and, to be honest, I was gagging for some action. I'd been on a few dates and read enough to know what not to do in bed, but I craved an experience with someone older. My girlfriends in the neighbourhood were great company but, try as I might, I just couldn't get worked up about them the way I did about Melinda. I'd taken to pulling myself off about twice a day thinking of her. And after a couple of weeks of this she started looking at me differently – taking her time to listen to me, her eyes slowly looking me over when I'd stand in the kitchen waiting for Jason in the mornings, or whenever I called round. I convinced myself I must have been sending out powerful signals of sexual energy, drawing her to me with all that concentrated thought.

Melinda didn't work, and she always looked stunning, with long, dark, lustrous hair and a great line in low-cut tops made of materials you wanted to stroke. She never looked brash or too old for her outfits; she had a grace about her that was ageless and her smile would melt my insides at twenty paces. The family was minted; they even had an electronic gate and a driveway. It was so different from the way my family lived. We had a nice house and stuff but it was always chaotic and noisy. Two younger sisters squealing on their karaoke machine and Dad endlessly drilling and doing DIY and my mum trying to keep a semblance of order. The Parrys' place was tranquil – Jason was their only kid – and Melinda spent most of her time refining the interior design. Even the floral displays were colour coordinated and bursting with life. Everything she came into contact with seemed to bloom into ripe sensuality.

I like to flatter myself with the notion that I orchestrated the seduction with my irresistible looks, but the most likely truth was that she was bored. When I think back to her body language, her carefully chosen expressions and her flirtatious laughter, it all seemed too obvious for anything to happen between us. But she was clever; it was a double bluff. I always know which of my friends are seeing which girl because, after months of giggling and whispering and teasing each other, there's suddenly silence between them – overcompensating to put their mates off the scent. It's the first sign someone's having sex. So I never read Melinda's hands-on behaviour as anything other than affection. The unthinkable happened out of the blue – and it kind of scuppered my theory. I now know that when your best mate's mum shows up to watch the cricket match her son is not even playing in, wearing a skirt that's short enough to be a low-slung belt, and settles herself in with a pair of binoculars, realisation should kick in that something unusual is afoot.

The Parrys' house is right near the school sports ground and, by early April, Melinda had started to watch me at practice, which I initially found odd and then occasionally distracting, and then a major turn-on. She told me she was interested in the game, which I found hard to believe, especially when she said I'd take at least five runs and score a half century of wickets. I laughed at her mix-up and tried to teach her the difference, but I could see it wasn't sinking in. But she was beginning to have an effect on my performance.

There was no getting Jason down there as a chaperone – he just wasn't interested in traditional sports, and I could hardly tell him what was beginning to blossom. In fact, there was no one I could talk to. I thought I was imagining things and I wasn't about to tell her to back off as I was enjoying the attention too much. I mean, what young man in his right mind would have had asked for protection from a sexy housewife he had fallen in love with?

She'd taken to giving me a lift home after practice, dropping me off and chatting innocently as you like with my mum and dad. I got a couple of sly comments from Scott, the team captain and the most worldly-wise of the lads, and I spotted the others giving her the occasional lustful glance, but they had no reason to be leery. Everything was innocent, in deed if not in thought. Summer was almost underway and she'd taken to wearing skimpier clothes. In the car I couldn't take my eyes off her legs and she wouldn't stop grazing my knee every time she changed gear.

The atmosphere had definitely become sexually charged. She wasn't just my mate's mum any more; she was a potential conquest. My first proper woman. She'd started to ask me about my girlfriends; what sort of women did I like; what pop stars and celebrities. I mentioned Angelina Jolie, only 'cos I couldn't really think of anyone else, but subconsciously I might have been thinking of Melinda when I said it. Melinda's about a foot shorter than AJ but the hair and the complexion are the same, and I prefer unusual, strong dark women to cutesy blondes. She smiled at that, and then came out with it: 'So, how many lovers have you had?' I fumbled. I faffed and mumbled. I shrugged and stuttered words that weren't in any vocabulary. Eventually I came out with the outrageous 'a few', although she knew I was being economical with the truth.

'I don't want you to be scared,' she said. 'You know I'm genuinely fond of you and care about you doing well...'

Yes, I was thinking. *And ... but ...*

'But the fact is I've become attracted to you. In the way that a woman is attracted to a man. I cannot bear not touching you any longer, Chris. You have become more than my son's friend.'

I knew the right thing would be to say thanks and get out of the car and leg it. Or text Jason and tell him his mum was losing it. Or give her my dad's number and say she'd be better off with a real man. But of course I did none of these. Instead I took a quick look in the rear view mirror, thought of all the wanking I'd done over her in the past year and, seeing no one I recognised, pulled her towards me by the shoulders and snogged her. My mate's mum.

And my world burst into a supernova of delight

as the reality of the situation filtered through to my consciousness. How cool was this! With my mouth still pressed to her lips I let my fingers stray to her breast. I nearly passed out with the joy and relief of finally laying hands on this goddess. I kept saying, 'Oh my God' and slapping a hand to my forehead. I was grinning like a loon and trying to remember whether I had packed any rubbers in my cricket bag. I was as nervous and excited as a shivering pup yet my ample rangy body felt as if it was expanding to giant size. I was becoming too big for the car. Not to mention the crotch of my cricket pants.

'Chris, listen to me,' she continued, 'I want to do it as much as you do. But we can't go to either of our houses and I'm not going to clamber into the back of the car with you.'

I was experiencing joy and desperation in equal measure. She wanted to 'do it' – but it wasn't going to happen this evening. When, then, when?

'No, of course not. I understand,' I managed to blurt out. 'It's just that I want to touch you so badly.'

My dick was flexing against the constraining cloth and Melinda had seized upon it. She must have known what agonising thrills were coursing through me. I practically had my head between her cleavage and I was not going to last long in that position, especially not with her touch firmly pressed on to my flesh. I had to get out of the car.

'I have to go, Melinda,' I said. 'I'm sure you know why. I'm not going to say anything to anyone.'

She smiled and caressed my cheek. 'I know you

won't. And I've got an idea. Something to improve your cricket,' she teased. 'If Rothermere wins the match, meet me behind the scoreboard just after the game, and I'll be there with a surprise for you.'

I didn't know whether to believe her or not – or indeed what to think after this extraordinary turn of events – but I walked briskly home with my cricket jumper in front of my crotch and a spring in my step. I couldn't wait to lock myself in the bathroom as soon as I got home and I lazily pulled on my cock in the bath thinking about Melinda's beautiful breasts as I shot a stream of vigorous sperm up on to the surrounding tiles.

Come the day of the tournament a couple of weeks later the sun was blazing and everyone's parents and friends were seated in deck chairs around the pitch. The lower years were serving refreshments to local dignitaries and the image was one of suburban serenity. Melinda was there with Jason and the sight of them together as mother and son turned my stomach into knots. Had she been shitting me about the special treat? Surely she wouldn't risk anything with Jason there. And my mum and dad were sat next to them. I had to put my love-struck thoughts out of my head and concentrate on the game – a limited 40-over innings each.

Levingtons won the toss and opted to bat first. Scott chose me to open the bowling and I gave the new ball a long slow rub along my thigh, hoping that Melinda was watching through her binoculars. The opposing side's team captain was first man at the crease and he was a big bastard for his age. I'd heard from Scott that he was South African, so I was already faced with a challenge. It wasn't like sending a ball down to Bradshaw or Neville from our own side: normal British lads who'd cut their teeth on the indoor nets at the local prep school. Guys like Levington's captain had the whole of veldt to practice in under a searing sun. Bugger.

I gave it my all and so did he – sending a couple of fours in the third over up to the boundary as our chaps slid their level best along the grass to stop the ball before it trundled into the refreshments tent, but failing. I'd managed to bowl one maiden over but Blankenfeld shamed me by hitting those two fours. After I'd bowled five overs Scott shifted position and I was moved into the slips. Crouching in the midday heat my thoughts kept jumping to what Melinda was planning, making polite conversation with my mum and dad and scoffing cheese and pickle sandwiches. I spent a few fretful minutes wondering what Jason would think if he knew what wheels had been put in motion. But he wouldn't know, would he? Because neither Melinda nor I were about to tell anyone what was occurring. If, indeed, anything was.

There was a sudden roar as the side of Blankenfeld's bat clipped a nice spin delivery from Neville. It rebounded at an awkward angle and my practice came into its own as I took one great leap for Rothermere College to stretch my right hand out at the perfect place. The leather orb smacked down nicely into my palm and their captain was dismissed for 28. It was a turning point. With the captain gone the rest of their lot fell like nine pins and we dispatched them for 92 all out.

It was back to the pav for refreshments and a consultation with the team for our innings tactics but my mind was on Melinda, and whether she'd seen my lucky catch. We must have looked the epitome of youthful vigour as we strode across the pitch, slapping each other on the back and showing congrats all round, exaggeratedly replaying the near misses and flukey triumphs. I caught sight of her with my dad, waving to me, and I flexed inside my cricket box, safe at least in the knowledge that if I got a hard-on it would be shielded by that essential cup of plastic that's protected a man's tackle and modesty since the game was invented.

Our innings in bat got off to a modest start, with Scott hitting safety strokes and notching up ones and twos nice and steady. Levington's bowling was a bit shoddy and, apart from their prize seam bowler, Haynes, setting up a couple of catches off our boys, we inched towards victory as the sun cast long shadows over the green. I went in as fourth man and determined to liven things up. After a frustrating start I got my chance on the final ball of the over when their bloke bowled short and I had time to really get behind my stroke. In a resounding crack, I was rewarded with the perfect sound and sensation of hitting the ball in the optimum part of the bat and I sent the ball flying over the boundary for the first six of the game.

The spectators got to their feet and their encouragement spurred me on to greater heights. As my partners changed through being caught out, and we suffered one LBW, I went on to realise that the game would be ours within the half hour, if I managed to keep my head and play it steady. Just as I predicted, their strategy fell apart under the onslaught of our tactical game and I began to feel as if I was in the right place at the right time. I wondered fleetingly if I'd ever feel like that when I went to university but I didn't have the luxury of idle reveries; we had a game to finish off. With two men on our side still to pad up and 80 runs on the scoreboard, I put my all into it. I was paid back in full, and as the minutes clocked by and the chances of Levington's taking any more wickets looking decidedly slim, victory was in sight.

The large white numbers came round on the scoreboard and we'd done it. Levington's were all bluff and bluster with their fancy South African batsman, but they couldn't play the long game. The cup was ours and my name would have a place in the school records. The spectators got to their feet and cheered and the headmaster made his cheery announcements over the loudspeaker system. As we walked back to the pavilion I waved my bat high in the air and felt like a young god. Then I heard my name being called and Melinda was at my side. She was nodding her head vigorously and mouthing me to join her. I mouthed back 'scoreboard' and she nodded. It wasn't easy to slip away so, to avoid suspicion, I went into the pavilion and shot out the back door so I wouldn't be noticed by the others. She was waiting for me for me in the appointed place.

* * *

I hadn't had time to shower, and yet she told me how good I smelt. It takes a real woman to appreciate the scent of schoolboy sweat. I bounded off in my grass-stained clothes with much haste. At least she allowed me time take off my box.

Before I knew what was happening she had dragged me into the allotments that back on to the sports ground. The college grounds cover a huge area and there are riding stables and a tennis club as well as an ancient stretch of woodland within easy reach. As we jogged across the allotment – over the patches of string beans and cabbages – one or two eager gardeners glanced our way and we nodded to them. They probably thought we were mother and son. I didn't dwell on the fact Melinda was more than twice my age. There was only now and this moment that I'd waited a good couple of years for. I wasn't about to put obstacles in front of my imminent pleasure.

Once we were out of sight of anybody she took my hand and we slipped lightly into the woods. Every crackle of every twig set my heart pounding. I was excited beyond a level I had ever experienced and nervous as hell. When Melinda ducked down into the undergrowth she gave me a flash of her brown legs and I couldn't wait to get my hands around them. She came to a stop by a small sheltered clearing surrounded by overgrown brambles, fell against a tree and spun round to face me as I advanced on her.

I must have looked incongruous in my sports gear – adrift from my teammates and intoxicated with lust and joy – the happy cricketer in the woods. I eased my hands around her tiny waist and she wriggled against me, feeling for me between my legs. She hooked a leg up around my thigh and then, for the first time, I made contact with her private parts. Even the feel of it – like a plump hot fruit – drove me near to the edge of letting go too soon. I needed the real thing and I hoped to all the gods that she wouldn't back out on me now.

I kissed her deeply, feeling electrified by my desire. I'd looked at a lot of porn on the net and had a good stash of magazines but that fabricated stuff can never convey the feeling of a woman's heat and the beguiling softness of her touch. Her tiny hand was rubbing me along the length of my extremely hard penis. She was cooing and smiling; telling me how big I was. After a minute of this I could stand it no longer.

'Can I?' I breathed raggedly into her ear, picking up on her lemony perfume.

'I think so,' she said. 'I mean, you are old enough, aren't you? Seventeen? I should have done this a year ago.'

'I think a year ago it would have been all over in the car the other day and I'd had to have done my own laundry again.'

She laughed and told me to kneel at her feet and pull her knickers down. With absolute determination not to press against the seam of my trousers too ardently I slowly prolonged the delicious agony – and the earthy scent of her womanliness drifted into the air and seduced me. I pressed my face to her sex and breathed gently on it, before taking my chances and allowing myself the thrill of poking my naughty little tongue between her lips. She began grinding her hips against me, clawing her fingers through my hair and telling me to work it faster.

At the same time I eased two fingers along her slit and was shocked by how damp she was. Which was nothing compared to the moisture that coated my hand as I slid into the silky interior, pressing my knuckles up against her pubic bone. I was in her at last – a dress rehearsal for the real thing that surely would be mine in a matter of minutes. I became more creative with my tongue, using its muscular dexterity to bring her to a climax as quickly as I could. I was worshipping her to be allowed my own release. But she was to have hers first – and oh my God did she go for it! If I hadn't have been so aroused by feeling her give under my ministrations, I might have been concerned that someone would hear us. But at that moment I didn't care; I had waited too long.

I was so hard by the time I managed to extricate myself from my white trousers that I was shaking with need. Melinda had sunk down the tree to squat on her haunches, and in that position she parted her knees to allow me to see her in all her glory. I stretched out an arm and aimed my thumb towards her clit. She seemed to like it so I rubbed her softly, feeling the warmth and moisture she had just oozed from her orgasm. I tilted her gently over on to her back, into the leaf mulch and ready for me. I nudged my cock against her, and I knew I would have to exercise supreme control not to spurt my hot liquid over her. The sight of her lying there with her wispy satin panties stretched between her knees and her ripe, plump lips glistening in the shadow between her thighs was a living porn tableau. I held myself tight in my hand, rubbing the slippy moisture that had seeped from the eye over my shaft. I was ready to blow.

I reached in my pocket for the condom but she told me not to worry about it; she was on the pill. And she then announced rather than asked, 'This is your first time, isn't it?'

At least she hadn't used the 'V' word. I nodded my head, unable to look her in the eyes. But she insisted I relax; that there was no shame.

'The first time should be a tribute. I want to feel you let go inside me. I want to feel the seed of a virgin. It's my first time, too. I've never taken a boy's cherry before.'

I felt a brief moment of panic but it didn't stop me; nothing would have. I wanted to come so badly. And then it was there; the first silky feel of her smooth moist slit on my dick was all it took to send me to heaven.

We looked into each other's eyes. She played the coquettish maiden, biting a finger and drawing her breath in sharply. She was driving me insane.

'Talk to me, Chris,' she said.

I didn't know what to say. I just kept telling her she was beautiful.

'I love it that you've still got your cricket whites on,' she continued. 'I've got a special thing about cricketers. I like to watch them slowly rub the ball along the inside of their thighs. I watched you do that earlier and it made me wet for you.'

It was her that was doing all the talking but I didn't mind.

'I was so ready for it when we were in the car. I knew I wouldn't take long to come. I loved it just now when you flicked your tongue into my cunt. This is your reward, Chris.'

That was it. I felt the molten fire build in my balls and began to push harder.

'Oh God,' I panted. 'Oh, that's it, I'm coming, I'm coming.'

And with my hands roaming over her breasts and the sound of the lewd words she had uttered in my ear still ringing in my consciousness as being such a very wrong thing for your mate's mum to say, there was an explosion of exquisite excitement as I let it all go inside her. To look up and stare directly into the face of my dad.

So now I'm sitting here biting my nails and feeling a mixture of elation at finally losing my V and terror at what he's going to do? Will he tell mum? Surely not! And Jason. Will he know about it? I did the only thing a boy would do, and legged it. I said thank you over and over to Melinda and sorry about twice that amount. They couldn't really blame me, could they? I was man of the match, after all.

Oh God, that's the front door. Oh Christ, Cavendish, you've really dropped yourself in it.

There's a knock at my door.

'Come in,' I croak, standing up ready to face the music and the wrath.

'Surprise!'

In fall Melinda and my dad. Dad's swigging from an open wine bottle and the pair of them look beside themselves with glee.

'What?' I begin. 'What's going on?'

'Look, son. Don't you worry. Nothing's going to happen. Mum doesn't know a thing.'

'And neither does Jason,' said Melinda.

'And that's the way it's going to stay?' I suggest.

'In one,' says Dad. 'The thing is, I was so determined to see your name on that cup, I knew that a little incentive would work wonders.'

'It was no chore, Bill,' says Melinda. 'He's a beautiful boy.' She looked at me with genuine affection, and the worry eased out of my body. But I was still confused.

'We'd better be getting back to the grounds, before there's any hoo-ha,' said Melinda.

'Chris needs to come back too, don't you, son? Mingle with the local nobs and celebrate with your team mates.'

'But, how...?'

'Look, let's just say me and your mum are a bit friendlier with a select few neighbours than we might have let on. You're going off to university and you'll have your fun. We need ours too, you know. What fun would there be in suburbia without a bit of swinging?'

'You mean, you and Melinda...?' I ventured.

'No, *you* and Melinda,' he said. 'We met socially recently at an informal group. I'm not going into details but let's say we were talking about what a shame it was that most young men have to fumble around with girls their own age when they're, you know, that age when they get all emotional and silly on them. What better than to revert to the ancient ways of a lovely older woman deflowering the young heroes of the village! And then we got to talking about the match. We'd had a few drinks and one thing led to another and so Melinda and I concocted a fiendish plan.'

He said it with such gusto. I guess he's always been a bit of an old pagan, with his fondness for real ale and Morris dancing. All that 'deflowering' stuff was pagan, after all, wasn't it? Not exactly sanctioned by the C of E.

'Let this be your summer solstice ceremony,' he said. 'So come back and take the cup for the college. You went into bat a boy, and you return to take the cup as a man!'

So now I'm standing by the pavilion, and the headmaster is holding the microphone to my dad as an old boy of the school to say a few words.

'I've waited years for this day,' he began.

And as the sun set over the pavilion and the sounds of glasses tinkled around the green, all was well with England and my future. I was beaming.

'And so have I, believe me,' I chipped in. 'So have I.'

Jan Bolton's short stories have appeared in numerous Wicked Words collections.

Kissing the Gunner's Daughter Fiona Locke

'Reporting for duty, sir,' Emily said, touching the brim of her cocked hat.

Sebastian gaped at her.

She stood stiffly to attention, keeping her eyes front as her twin brother circled her, scrutinising her. The Royal Navy uniform was a perfect fit. The bum-freezer jacket and buff waistcoat hid her feminine curves well. Below the stiff turnback collar, her dainty neck was disguised by the black stock and white shirt-frill. Not even the tight white breeches betrayed her true sex.

Her dark hair was pulled back away from her face and tied with a velvet ribbon. But the bicorn hat would draw the eye away from her delicate facial features. And Emily knew that life at sea would harden her. She could never pass for a grown man, of course. But in Sebastian's uniform she looked every inch a midshipman in His Majesty's navy. A young gentleman in training to become an officer.

Sebastian Vane had no stomach for adventure, despite their father's ambition that he command a King's ship one day. Conversely, Emily deeply resented the thought of being sent to finishing school while her brother fought glorious battles against the French. At eighteen, she was a burden on their father, as she had no intention of marrying. She refused to condemn herself to a life of domestic duty, and she skilfully alienated every potential suitor her father chose for her.

'Will I pass?' she asked, pitching her voice a little lower.

Unable to speak, Sebastian simply nodded his head in admiration. 'I think you just might.'

'Thank you.' Emily turned to regard herself in the cheval mirror. She and her brother might be satisfied with her appearance, but it was Lieutenant Trevelyan she must convince.

She was nervous, but she did her best to conceal it from Sebastian, lest he change his mind. The twins had traded places before and no one had known the difference. But this time there was no going back.

Lieutenant Trevelyan was the son of a post captain who had known the Vane family for years. The twins' father, a prominent member of parliament, had prevailed upon the captain to get Sebastian a midshipman's place aboard HMS *Nemesis*. He thought some time in the navy was just what the lad needed.

The redoubtable young lieutenant had dined with the Vanes many times and Emily always pleaded with him to share his stories about life at sea. Trevelyan naturally assumed she wanted to hear about brave victories and he indulged her with accounts of capturing French and Spanish prize ships.

She listened politely; however, her interests were a little less romantic. And when Trevelyan happened onto the topic of naval discipline her heart gave a little leap. She found it remarkable that the men subject to such harsh punishments did not resent it. But Trevelyan assured her that it was necessary for maintaining order on board a ship. The men would sneer at a captain who was lax in his discipline and think him soft. The cat-o'-nine-tails wasn't used indiscriminately, but it was used often. However, that was a punishment only for common seamen. Midshipmen were treated differently.

Sebastian dreaded any talk about his impending naval career, but Emily couldn't get enough. She loved hearing about the midshipmen most of all.

The 'young gentlemen' were not put to the lash. Instead they were punished with a rattan cane. Trevelyan told them once about a young gentleman who had failed to batten the hatch to the powder magazine properly. This was a serious oversight and Trevelyan ordered him below deck and sent for the boatswain. The lad was bent over a cannon and caned severely across the seat of his breeches, which offered scant protection. The position was known as 'kissing the gunner's daughter'. The image had been indelibly imprinted in Emily's mind.

'He was most attentive to his duties after that,' Trevelyan said with a meaningful glance at Sebastian.

The boy looked forlornly at his untouched dinner.

Emily pressed her thighs together.

Another evening Emily had the lieutenant to herself in the library. As usual, she insisted on stories and he obliged. She had to rein in her fascination as she teased out the details and nuances that intrigued her, grateful that her brother had gone to bed.

Occasionally an even more severe punishment than caning was ordered. Then the miscreant's hands would be tied together underneath the barrel of the cannon and he would be flogged on the bare bottom with the boy's cat, a smaller cat-o'-nine-tails made of whipcord. Trevelyan explained that the miscreant was required to make his own cat, which the first lieutenant inspected personally.

His authoritarian voice made Emily squirm with secret delight as she pictured herself in the place of the unfortunate who had displeased him. And late at night, alone in her bed, Emily replayed her fantasies while her fingers strayed inside her nightdress. It was the stern face of Lieutenant Trevelyan she saw when her body writhed and bucked in guilty pleasure.

Her punishment fantasies centred around Trevelyan disciplining her as a boy. But sometimes her struggles caused her to reveal her feminine charms to him. He never broke stride; with a rakish grin, he told her he'd known she was a young woman all along. Then he took her to his cabin and had his wicked way with her.

But this was no longer merely fantasy. What would he do if he did discover her true sex? A man who impersonated an officer would be hanged from the yardarm. But there was nothing in the *Articles of War* about punishments for ladies. The lieutenant would have to devise his own.

Emily gazed at the midshipman in the mirror. She cut a dashing figure in the uniform and looked quite a handsome lad, if a little soft. That would not earn her any lenience from Trevelyan, though. It was that very softness he was charged with reforming.

Closing her eyes, Emily forgot her brother's presence as she indulged her favourite fantasy.

In her mind she faced Lieutenant Trevelyan nervously as he delivered a scathing reprimand about her misconduct. He stood before her, an imposing figure in his long frock coat and fore-and-aft hat. Though she knew it was the boatswain who administered punishments, Emily liked to imagine the lieutenant himself caning her. Perhaps her misbehaviour would be such that only an officer was qualified to address it.

'The navy, Mr Vane, is founded on discipline.'

Emily flinched as he showed her the cane and tapped the cannon with it.

'You know the position, boy.'

Trembling, Emily bent over the cannon. Trevelyan slowly unfastened her breeches and peeled them down, exposing the quivering pale flesh of her bottom. She knew that the other midshipmen would hear the cuts of the cane up on deck, but she would not give them the satisfaction of hearing her cry out.

She held her breath as Trevelyan raised the cane . . .

'Emily?'

At the sound of her brother's voice she shook herself out of her reverie, flushing deeply. 'Sorry,' she murmured. 'I was just thinking of the lieutenant.'

Sebastian made a face. He couldn't understand her lust for adventure at all. The prospect of going to sea with Trevelyan terrified him. But their father would not be persuaded against it. It would make a man of him.

Suddenly, Sebastian bit his lip. 'I don't know, Em,' he said. 'Someone is bound to find out.'

Emily met her brother's eye with confidence. 'Why should they? I'll be careful.'

'I couldn't bear the disgrace if we were discovered. Father would die.'

'You mustn't worry.'

A light breeze stirred the curtains, bringing with it the sound of an approaching carriage.

The twins froze, listening. Sure enough, the horses' hooves stopped just outside.

'He's here,' Sebastian whispered, apprehensive.

A delicious shudder ran through Emily, tickling her like tiny feet scurrying over her skin. 'Come, Sebastian. We don't have much time.'

She snatched her chemise and corset from the bed and helped Sebastian into them. He gasped as she pulled the laces of the corset tight. Emily smiled. There was some satisfaction to be had in inflicting the torments of feminine undergarments on a male. Tomorrow he'd have to fasten the stays himself.

The twins had been rehearsing for weeks, and

Sebastian's slight frame wore his sister's clothes well. His transformation was even more striking than Emily's. He was lost inside the heavy brocade gown and bonnet.

'Take a look,' she said, gesturing at the mirror.

Sebastian crossed the room in three awkward, boyish strides.

'You haven't been practising,' Emily lamented. 'You must remember to walk as I showed you. Take small steps. Everyone waits for a lady.'

He nodded, swallowing nervously.

'Now show me your curtsey.'

He managed a clumsy plié.

'I expect it will have to do,' she said with a sigh. 'But you must work on it.'

Sebastian nodded. 'And you must remember to stand with your feet apart. Let your elbows go. Don't be graceful.' He examined her hands doubtfully. 'And get these dirty as soon as possible. They're far too ladylike.'

Emily's stomach fluttered in a sudden frisson of fear. There were so many ways she could slip up. Then what would she do? Throw herself on the mercy of the captain?

'It's best if you don't come down,' she said. 'I've been brooding all week about Father sending you to sea, so he won't be expecting to see me. Just stay up here – as me – and mope in my room. Refuse to go down tomorrow as well. Stay here sulking and practise being me.'

Sebastian laughed. 'We're both mad, you realise. Absolutely mad.'

'Ah, yes, but it's the adventure of a lifetime. Just

imagine if I should pass the examination for lieutenant.'

'You could be a captain one day.'

'Or an admiral.'

'And what shall I do?' Sebastian mused. 'Make up with one of your spurned suitors and marry?' He batted his eyes coquettishly and they dissolved into laughter. But a sombre mood soon descended. This was the last time they would see each other for a long time.

'Just mind you don't find yourself on the wrong side of the lieutenant,' Sebastian warned, his face pale. 'He won't brook any weakness.'

Emily blushed and looked down at her shoes. The candlelight shone in the gleaming buckles. Her strange obsession with discipline was the one thing she'd been unable to confide in her brother. Rather than confessing that the prospect thrilled her, she feigned nonchalance. 'Oh, he doesn't frighten me,' she said with a plucky grin.

Suddenly, they heard their father, calling for Sebastian.

Sebastian straightened Emily's hat and dusted down her coat. After one last look he handed her his books and sextant. 'Good luck, Em,' he said. 'I shall miss you.'

'And I shall miss you.' Tears threatened to well in her eyes and she blinked them back. It wouldn't do for a future captain of Nelson's navy to be seen weeping like a girl.

'Will you write to me?' Sebastian asked.

Emily drew herself up proudly. 'Of course.' She

took his hand and kissed it, giving a little bow. 'My sweet sister.'

Then with a final glance in the mirror, she hurried off to meet her fate.

Emily had studied the books with diligence – Norie's *Epitome of Navigation* and Clarke's *Complete Handbook of Seamanship*. She was familiar with much that a midshipman was meant to know, in theory, at least. But she was completely unprepared for the bewildering reality of it all. She marvelled at the array of rigging towering above her. Everywhere there was frantic activity that would seem like chaos to an outsider. Orders were bellowed from one end of the ship to the other. Men scrambled up and down the ratlines without so much as a downward glance. She watched as the hands aloft loosed the headsails and topsails and got the ship under way.

She could barely contain her excitement as the *Nemesis* left land behind and headed out into the ocean. But the unceasing corkscrew roll of the frigate soon took its toll on some of the new midshipmen, who staggered about with ashen faces while the seasoned crew looked smug. Emily was glad she was not alone in that particular misery. And most of the lads seemed to be suffering worse than she was.

In the days that followed, Emily often caught sight of Lieutenant Trevelyan, but he paid her no mind. She watched him whenever she could, straining to hear his voice. He issued orders with a natural authority that made her legs weak. Men touched their forelocks to him and scurried off to do his bidding. The dampness between her legs could easily make her forget she was supposed to be a boy.

Trevelyan stood on the quarterdeck with his feet well apart and his hands clasped behind his back. Emily was still learning to balance on the pitching ship, but the lieutenant stood as solid as the mainmast. She longed for an excuse to approach him, to speak to him, if only to impart some trivial bit of information and await his orders.

'You, boy!'

She jumped.

It was Wagstaffe, the oldest inhabitant of the midshipmen's berth. At twenty-five, his chances of making lieutenant were slipping away, and it did not improve his temper.

It took a few moments for Emily to realise he was addressing *her*.

'The master wants to know why you aren't at lessons with the rest of us.'

'I couldn't find my way, sir,' she mumbled, lowering her head. She regretted her show of submission instantly. Sebastian had instructed her to make eye contact.

'Lost, are you, snotty?' he sneered.

Emily had never before been spoken to in such a manner and she had no idea how she was meant to respond. That was one thing Clarke's *Seamanship* couldn't tell her. But she screwed up her pluck, raised her head and pushed past him. 'Beg pardon, sir,' she said gruffly.

Behind her she heard him laugh. Her face

burned. She was annoyed with herself. Any show of weakness would make her a victim among her shipmates. She had to be more assertive.

When she eventually found the others and took a seat, the sailing master glowered at her. Then he called on her to tell him the equation relating the leeway to the trim of the sails. He let her flounder with tangents and cotangents for nearly a minute before silencing her disgustedly. Blake, a younger midshipman, was only too happy to supply the correct answer, smiling loftily at the unfortunate Mr Vane.

She glared back at him and was immensely pleased with herself when Blake looked away, abashed.

But her triumph was short-lived. The next day the master berated her for miscalculating the ship's latitude. Most of the others got it wrong too, but she was already in his bad books from the day before. Emily loathed the tedious lessons. Navigation was going to be her downfall, she was certain. And the endless hours of inactivity dampened her spirits. When would they get to fight?

The morning's lesson was finally over and Emily was relieved to be left alone to study. She peered out over the waves, squinting through the eyepiece of her sextant. She found the sun in the half-silvered mirror and slid the index arm round carefully until the image was superimposed on the horizon. Clamping the sextant, she read the angle off the scale. Simple enough. It was the calculations that defeated her. Sebastian had warned her that her mathematical ical skills would need improving, but sines and cosines were not her strong point. She had been so impetuous about the enterprise that she simply hadn't given trigonometry much thought.

'So what's our latitude, Mr Vane?'

She jumped at the familiar voice, nearly dropping her sextant. 'I haven't done the calculations yet, sir,' she said.

Trevelyan gestured for her to continue, but he made no move to leave. 'Very well, then. Carry on.'

Emily grew even more nervous. She'd never get it right with him standing over her.

She tried to shoot the sun the second time, but her fingers trembled so much that she couldn't hold the instrument still. The sun was a jumpy golden gash in the mirrors, but she clamped it anyway and looked at the angle. Then she realised she'd forgotten the angle of the first sight. She'd have to take it again and risk his disapproval. Then there were the calculations and corrections, which she had yet to be successful with. She suspected her position line would be off by several degrees.

Trevelyan stood immobile, but Emily could sense his growing impatience. She began to panic. 'Sir, forgive me, I . . . I'm still learning the calculations.'

He frowned. 'My boy, you should have learned those before setting foot on board. You were meant to be studying these many weeks past.' His voice was strict and unsparing. He had been charged with the duty of making a man of this delicate boy. No one knew better than Emily that he took his responsibilities very seriously.

'Yes, sir,' Emily said, crestfallen. She had no excuse to offer him.

'The sailing master thinks you lack application.' He held out his hand for the sextant and for a moment she feared he would tell her she had no place on board, that they would set her down in the next English port. But instead he put the eye-piece to his eye and took the sight himself.

He read out the angle and Emily noted it. He took the second angle and looked at her enquiringly.

'Now, Mr Vane, how do we combine the two sightings?'

That much she could do. Sixty degrees minus the second angle should be equal to the first. But what came next? The index error? She searched her mind, but came up blank.

Frightened as she was, she thrilled at his near-ness as he stood looking down on her. She fixed on the impeccable cut of his uniform. She could see the ropes twisting round the anchors on every single gilt button.

He had asked her a question. Oh, yes. The sight-ings. Emily searched her mind for an answer. She wanted desperately to please him, to prove herself worthy. But she was completely lost. True, she had neglected her studies; but her desire was also clouding her ability to concentrate.

His ice-blue eyes glittered. 'Perhaps I should have young Blake assist you.'

The comment rankled. She had been feeling so much better after staring Blake down the day before. Now he was eroding what little confidence she'd acquired. Bristling, Emily held her tongue.

'Come on, Mr Vane. Any of the master's mates could have done these calculations by now.'

'Then perhaps the master's mates should do it, sir,' she blurted out. 'Surely an officer has more important things to do than play with numbers.'

She regretted it the instant she said it. Trevelyan's face hardened and she realised the enormity of her mistake.

She swallowed. 'I'm sorry, sir. I . . . forgot myself.'

Trevelyan was eyeing her severely.

Her cheeks burned. 'Sir, I . . .' What could she say?

'That will be quite enough from you,' he said softly.

Her head lowered, she stared fixedly at a coil of rope at her feet. She felt light-headed and if she'd been wearing a corset she might have swooned. Emily had to remind herself that she was no longer a lady. When the silence became unbearable she raised her head to face him.

'Report to the gundeck at eight bells in the afternoon watch.'

Blanching, Emily struggled to keep her voice steady. 'Aye aye, sir,' she said, touching her hat with unsteady fingers.

The lieutenant turned and walked away down the deck.

She recalled Trevelyan saying once that he liked to be present when he had ordered punishment. He said it reinforced the formality. She was frightened, but also exhilarated. The shadow of a smile touched her lips at the thought of him seeing her caned. There was the familiar tingling heat between her legs and she had to glance down to make sure there was nothing outwardly visible. The wetness felt conspicuous in her tight breeches. She tugged gently at her waistband, moaning a little at the pressure of the seam against her crotch.

The forenoon watch had barely begun; she had several hours yet to wait. She looked around to see if anyone might have been within earshot, but she was alone. Perhaps no one else had heard the exchange. Then they wouldn't know to listen for the telltale swish of the bosun's rattan. She could hope.

She busied herself as best she could, trying not to think about what was coming. But every time the ship's bell rang out her pulse quickened. In her head she heard the lieutenant's pronouncement over and over again. She couldn't concentrate on anything but her impending punishment.

At ten minutes before eight bells, the new officer of the watch came on deck. It was time. Emily didn't want Trevelyan to get to the gundeck before her.

She forced herself to hold her head up, in disgrace but not dishonour. Her heart banged behind her ribs and her legs wavered like a drunken sailor's as she made her way below deck.

The gundeck normally bustled with activity and noise. Now it was deserted. Trevelyan must have given orders. Emily was thankful for that. While witnesses might strengthen her resolve to take the punishment bravely, she didn't know how she would face them afterwards. She stood beside one of the twelve-pounders, caressing its cold body. It was so much larger than she had imagined back home. Very soon she would be bent over it, suffering under the cane.

The air was warm and heavy and Emily felt the back of her neck begin to prickle. For a moment she regretted taking Sebastian's place here, but she shook off the thought disgustedly. She had wanted adventure. She had *demanded* it. Now that she faced her fantasies at last, she had no choice but to follow through.

She lifted her head proudly. She was a King's officer. If she flinched at the prospect of a caning, how could she ever face the French in battle? Or look in the mirror?

In the distance she heard the ship's bell herald the end of the watch. Then the sound of boots on the ladder. This was it. She took several deep breaths to calm herself. No one would know how much she secretly wanted this.

Lieutenant Trevelyan appeared with Harmwell, the bosun. Emily flinched when she saw the stout malacca cane he carried. She lowered her head, hoping they would take it for penitence and not fear.

Trevelyan's stern voice boomed in the confined space. 'Mr Vane seems to think navigation is beneath him. But I think we have the means to teach him some humility. Haven't we, Mr Vane?'

'Yes, sir' was the only answer to that. Emily thought she would melt.

'Twelve good hard strokes, I think, Mr Harmwell.'

'Aye aye, sir.'

Trevelyan nodded solemnly towards the cannon and Emily steeled herself as she turned towards it. She removed her hat and laid it aside. Then she placed her hands on the cannon. With her legs together she bent forwards at the waist, sideways over the gun. She knew she must bear the indignity.

'Not like that, lad,' came Harmwell's gruff voice. 'Along the gun. One leg either side.'

She choked back a gasp. She hadn't pictured it like that! The idea of wrapping her legs around the barrel seemed indecent. It was the way a gentleman rode a horse. But she obeyed, straddling the cold metal and stretching herself out along its length, presenting her bottom for the cane.

At that moment she wished she could see Trevelyan's face. What expression did he wear? Stern indifference? Sadistic pleasure? She didn't dare turn round to see.

Emily flinched as she felt the malacca touch her bottom, measuring the first stroke. She tensed in anticipation, waiting. An age passed before Trevelyan gave the command for the punishment to begin.

The cane drew back and she heard a low deep whistle as it cut through the air. It sliced into her bottom with a loud *thwack*! She was unprepared for the force of the stroke and she yelped, more out of surprise than pain.

'One,' Harmwell counted.

The sting began to bloom in a line across her bottom and she fought the urge to reach back and clutch the burning flesh. Her breeches offered no protection at all. The position pulled them deep into the cleft of her bottom, separating her cheeks. A perfect target.

Emily gritted her teeth for the next stroke and managed to stay silent as it painted a second burning stripe across her posterior.

'Two.'

The third stroke forced a sharp intake of breath and she clung to the cannon as tightly as she could. Her arms trembled with the effort and her hands were clammy against the metal. In her fantasies, Trevelyan had usually tied her wrists together. That would be a mercy now. The possibility of disgracing herself by leaping out of position was a challenge she hadn't counted on. Sweat trickled down her face and she panted, waiting for the next stroke.

Again the bosun's rattan met her tender bottom. She hissed through her teeth, determined to stifle her cries. Trevelyan was watching; she could not bear his reproach.

'Four.'

Harmwell's dutiful counting was strangely humbling. It was clear he got no pleasure from this; he was simply obeying orders. It was inexplicably erotic. The lieutenant's power over her was absolute.

As the caning continued, Emily found herself floating, as though watching from outside herself. She could take this; perhaps she was toughening up. Trevelyan was doing what he had promised her father he would do: making a man of her. There was something poetic about that.

A particularly hard stroke forced another cry from her and she cursed herself for her weakness. She heard the bosun counting the strokes, but the numbers meant nothing to her. Intense as the pain was, Emily felt invigorated. It was the ultimate challenge. The proving ground. This was what she'd wanted. Her beloved lieutenant was having her flogged for insubordination and he was overseeing the punishment personally. Had he been waiting for the opportunity as well, to do his duty by the faint-hearted boy?

Harmwell counted ten and Emily breathed deeply, pacing herself for the final two strokes. She could imagine the spectacle she made – her bottom turned well up, her tight breeches inviting the sting of the cane. Trevelyan had no idea he was watching a *girl's* bottom and the secret knowledge gave Emily a lewd little thrill. She squeezed her thighs against the cannon, stimulating herself as the penultimate stroke fell.

'Eleven,' counted Harmwell.

Emily held her breath for the last stroke, but the lieutenant interrupted.

'The final stroke,' he said, 'is always the hardest. Make this one count, Mr Harmwell.'

'Aye aye, sir.'

She sensed the cane drawing back and she gritted her teeth, squeezing her eyes shut tightly.

The last stroke slashed through the air and into her bottom, its impact echoing in her head like a musket shot. She was lost in a strange haze of pain spiced with pleasure. It was not unlike being drunk. Her body was tingling and the throbbing in her sex was almost unbearable. She longed to rub herself against the cold metal of the cannon, to tighten her legs round it until the pleasure exploded within her. But she would have to wait. She would take care of it later that night, in her hammock in the midshipmen's berth.

The bosun gave a little cough and Emily shook her head to clear it.

'You may stand up, Mr Vane,' said the lieutenant.

She slid to her feet and stood up shakily. Then she raised her eyes to look Trevelyan in the face. It was important to regain her dignity.

'Have you revised your opinion of navigation, Mr Vane?' the lieutenant asked.

'Yes, sir. I most certainly have, sir.'

He eyed her sternly for a few moments before addressing the bosun. 'Leave us, Mr Harmwell.'

'Aye aye, sir.'

They were alone. The silence quickly became oppressive. A bead of sweat rolled down her face and she dared not rub it away.

At last he spoke. 'Well, Mr Vane?'

Was it her imagination or had he emphasised the 'Mr'?

'S-sir?'

'Look at me when you're spoken to, lad.'

Emily tried not to blush, but it was impossible. Warmth flooded her face as she raised her eyes.

The lieutenant looked as austere as ever, yet there was a strange light in his eyes. 'Did that satisfy your curiosity?'

She swallowed. 'My – curiosity, sir?'

'Yes, your curiosity. Or have you forgotten our conversations in your father's library?'

Horrified, Emily lowered her head. She didn't know what to say.

The silence was broken by a harsh bark of laughter and she looked up, startled.

'You took that as well as any boy,' said Trevelyan, smiling broadly. 'I had my suspicions from the first, but your insubordination gave you away. Your brother would never have dared.'

Emily turned scarlet. 'I don't know what to say, sir.'

'You might thank me.'

'Thank you, sir.'

He nodded in acknowledgment. 'And now I should like to examine Mr Harmwell's handiwork.'

She blinked. 'Sir?'

Trevelyan gestured at the cannon. 'We'll have your breeches down, Emily.'

Amazed that she could possibly flush any deeper, she hesitated.

The lieutenant's expression grew severe again and he drew himself up. 'That was an order, Mr Vane.'

She gulped. 'Aye aye, sir.'

Then she turned away and her hands fluttered to her waist to unfasten her breeches. She looked nervously down the length of the gundeck.

'We're alone,' Trevelyan reassured her. 'Continue.'

It was so strange, baring herself like this before a man. She moved as though in a dream state, undoing the buttons at her knees. Her breeches pooled round her ankles. She'd done this often enough in her fantasies, but the reality was embarrassing, excruciating.

'Back in position,' Trevelyan ordered.

Emily did as she was told and her breeches slid down over her shoes. With her bottom on display and her bare thighs wrapped lewdly around the gun, the position was positively obscene. She moaned in exquisite shame as she lowered her forehead to the cannon. The barrel seemed warmer now and its hard surface pressed into her exposed sex.

She gave a little cry of surprise when she felt Trevelyan's hand against her bottom. His fingers traced the marks left by the cane and she shuddered at his touch.

'A commendable job,' he pronounced. 'Our Mr Harmwell has a strong arm.'

'Yes, sir,' Emily said with a gulp.

The lieutenant continued to examine the marks – slowly, thoroughly. He cupped her cheeks in his hands and squeezed firmly, making her gasp. The blood pounded in her head and again she felt faint. Then his fingers did the unthinkable. They slipped down along her crease and in between her legs.

Instinctively, Emily cried out and reached behind to shield herself, rising up out of her position.

'Oh, no,' chided the lieutenant, smacking her smartly on her tender backside. 'Stay where you are.'

Mortified, she obeyed.

'Perhaps you need restraining,' he suggested.

Her ears burned at those words. Out of the

corner of her eye she saw him reach for a coil of rope. Her breathing grew shallow as he crouched beside her and tied her wrists beneath the barrel, so that she embraced the cannon. Then he resumed his examination.

His skilful hands explored her sex, probing and fondling the slick folds. Emily stiffened and made a little whimper. But she didn't protest; she didn't dare risk breaking the spell.

The ropes let her imagine that this was just another part of her punishment. She pulled at them to reassure herself that she was truly at his mercy.

His fingers described careful little circles over and around the bud of her sex and she gasped at his expert stimulation. She hadn't known such ecstasy was possible. Her mouth opened in a soundless moan as the attentive fingers slipped inside her. The pain in her bottom had subsided to a dull pulse that mirrored the throbbing in her sex. She writhed wantonly as his fingers worked in and out of her, making her body jerk with pleasure.

Emily imagined that she was being caned again, this time bound naked to the grating up on deck. The entire crew stood watching as the lieutenant painted stripes across her disobedient bottom, counting dispassionately while she yelped and writhed in delirious torment.

When he withdrew his fingers, she squeezed her legs tightly around the gun, protesting with a petulant whimper.

But he wasn't finished with her. Again his fingers slid inside where she was warm and hungry. And this time his other hand caressed her as well, spreading her open and tweaking her little nub, hard. His attentions elicited gasps of alternating pleasure and pain and Emily threw her head back, arching against him, urging his fingers deeper inside her.

She was climbing fast, straining violently at the ropes, drowning in the liberation of total surrender. All at once the climax overtook her and the blood pounding in her ears sounded like the firing of the ship's guns.

For a long time neither of them said a word. Emily hung limply over the cannon, exhausted and panting. Trevelyan untied her hands. She stood on unsteady legs as she put her breeches back on and replaced her cocked hat.

'I hope you don't think that's the end of the matter,' he said gravely.

Misunderstanding, Emily's eyes widened. 'Oh, sir, you wouldn't tell the captain . . .'

Trevelyan gave her a conspiratorial smile. 'Probably not. I expect we can come to some arrangement. We can discuss it tonight. Report to my cabin at two bells in the first watch.'

Emily flushed. She felt her sex moistening again at the prospect. 'Aye aye, sir.'

'Navigation is important, Mr Vane,' he said. 'But action at close quarters is the true test of any officer.'

Fiona Locke's short stories have appeared in numerous Wicked Words collections. Her first novel, *Over the Knee*, is published by Nexus Enthusiast.